Jack Daniels on the Rocks

Michael Zielinski

To Pat,

Michael Zielinski

Dedication

To my beautiful wife Janice for all her love and support.

Chapter 1

John Daniels sat in the solitude of his office, sipping Scotch while getting sick -- of himself.

Well, sort of. It wasn't as if he were undergoing a midlife crisis. Because, at 57, he was a couple exits past middle age unless he could somehow live to 114. And criminal defense attorneys seldom have a shelf life approaching that. Yet the clock was ticking louder than a jackhammer on a long suppressed dream that threatened to light up his psyche and blow up the life that he knew.

Daniels was a prominent lawyer in Miller County, PA where the city of Braxton annually ranked dubiously high in the national crime statistics. The Greater Braxton area had plenty of bad guys, some of whom looked like good guys after Daniels gave them a legal shampoo and got them off despite their dastardly misdeeds. Daniels was a devout believer in the justice system, but pray tell there were times when he grew weary of wallowing in the criminal muck. He gave every case his all, but he knew many of his clients were scumbags who had guilt written across their foreheads until his courtroom magic washed it off. But the process couldn't wash away the hollow feeling inside Daniels that while justice may not be blind it definitely had cataracts. With Braxton's murder rate being rather robust, too many men with blood on their hands had dialed John Daniels' number, which had stained his soul to a degree.

"Damn, I need to lighten up," Daniels said aloud to himself the evening after a jury had found his latest client, a 21-year-old mother of four, innocent of second-degree murder in the fatal shooting of her latest live-in boyfriend of the month. Daniels had done a superb job of convincing the jury that his client had fired in self-defense even though her boyfriend had done nothing more aggressive toward her than raise his voice from across the room. His legal practice was flourishing and Daniels lived an affluent life in suburban Philmont. He was at the pinnacle of his profession, at least on the local level. But he was personally unfulfilled. He was bankrupt emotionally. His family life had vanished when his beloved wife had died of breast cancer several years earlier. She was busy in her career as a CPA and they had never found the time to have children. Daniels filled his private time with sports -- playing golf, although a cranky back had crimped both his fun and swing to a degree, and watching football and basketball. He rarely dated, even though he was tall, trim and distinguished and could have passed for 37 if it were not for the robust silver specks in an otherwise impressive head of hair. He had been so connected to his late wife Kate that he couldn't sustain any long-term interest in another woman. Since a connection to a ghost can be only so fulfilling and Daniels had no immediate plans to join Kate in the next world, he was lonelier than a hooker on Thanksgiving.

Late at night he found himself crafting rock melodies and lyrics by the light of a bottle of Scotch. The true passion of his life at this juncture was rock music. Classic rock. He listened to it constantly. In the office, even when working. In the car. At home, even while watching sports. At the gym. The only thing he knew better than the lyrics to classic rock songs was the Pennsylvania criminal code. At times he daydreamed he would have been happier had he become a rock star instead of an attorney. Granted, he probably would have been dead from drugs but the job stress would have been substantially less. He really had never confided this to anybody but Kate. And she thought he had rocks in his head -- so he buried the dream in the cellar of his soul.

Still, his desire to rock on became so powerful in him it burst and became a need.

And then John Daniels, the conservative defense attorney, sat bolt upright in his chair as if someone had just stuck a javelin up his ass.

"I can be a vocalist in a local cover band," he almost sang, knowing that he had talent that was shouting to be heard.

Then he laughed.

"Yeah, that will sure help my credibility in the courtroom," he said aloud. "And I gotta stop talking to myself."

John Daniels seldom talked aloud to himself. But he did sing to himself. And he had a great voice. The deep, rich voice he used as such a powerful instrument in the courtroom morphed into a baritone that sounded hauntingly like Jim Morrison of The Doors.

"It's time for Jack Daniels," he said aloud once again.

John Daniels had been Jack Daniels through law school. Even though he didn't like drinking Jack Daniels, he loved the name. When he was a star quarterback and shooting guard at Braxton High and Paxton College, which sits just a few blocks down Moss Street from his high school, the sportswriters at the *Braxton Bugle* had more fun with his name than grown men with their clothes on had a right to be.

Daniels poured himself some more Scotch and picked up the *Weekender* section of the *Braxton Bugle* to scan what bands were playing at what local clubs that Friday night.

"Time to rock on," Daniels smiled, breaking into a few self-rewritten lyrics of The Doors' *Alabama Song (Whiskey Bar)* in his otherwise deserted office.

I don't know the way
To any whiskey bar

And I know why
And I know why

Chapter 2

Daniels looked into his bedroom mirror and frowned as if he had just inhaled a gross fart.

He was getting dressed to scout some cover bands at local clubs and his casual dress was too much John Daniels and not enough Jack Daniels. After all, a rock singer can't look like an accountant or a dentist who was at a jazz concert. His long-sleeved dress shirt and khakis screamed Too Corporate like a wailing guitar. From a fashion standpoint, he simply had no street cred as a rocker. Then again, he knew he would look like a total jerk in a crummy T-shirt and torn jeans. His next shopping trip would have to be more thought-out than the D-Day invasion of Normandy.

For now, he decided to live with what he had on and go to Blind Hermit's Tavern in the sticks and then maybe the Beer Bucket in town -- hoping he didn't get lost going to the former and didn't get shot going to the latter. With some vintage Stones blaring *Gimme Shelter* in his ears, good fortune and his GPS landed him at Blind Hermit's Tavern. When he walked in, the place was rocking with people who mostly seemed younger and cooler to Daniels. Suddenly he felt as if he must have looked like Ben Franklin to everybody. That, of course, was his – Daniels', not Franklin's -- self-conscious perception. To the folks in the bar who may have noticed him, he looked like a conservatively dressed George Clooney, a little too distinguished-looking to rock out with the Pigs of Deception, who were adequately but certainly not spectacularly covering Led Zeppelin classics. Daniels squeezed up to the bar and finally flagged down a bartender after waving his arm until his rotator cuff started to fray just a bit.

"What do you want, pal?" barked the bartender, sporting a beer gut that spilled into another zip code and a long ponytail even though hair had deserted the top of his dome.

For a moment, Daniels almost ordered his standard Johnnie Walker Blue Label Scotch on the rocks. Then he caught himself.

"Jack Daniels on the rocks," he shouted through the din, a surge of metamorphosis shooting down his spinal column. After he got his drink, Daniels moved to a table in the rear and soaked in the atmosphere. It was a bar where the patrons took their drinking seriously. They were often buy-a-vowel drunk, spewing cuss words and looking to fight. And the men were sometimes worse.

Daniels was there on a scouting mission, to see if he could project himself actually performing in a local club. Since the lead singer in Pigs of Deception looked more like a dorky mechanic than Robert Plant and had a shrill voice, Daniels knew after the band's set had concluded that he could do THIS - - that John could morph into Jack. The Jack had gone down well and after sauntering up to the bar for a second drink, he spotted the Pigs of Deception vocalist talking to a heavyset blonde who had bigger arms than an NFL lineman and a chest big enough to play the Super Bowl on if the players were willing to slide downhill. Daniels walked up to him for a chat, but made a mental note to be casual and not sound as if he were talking to a guy on the witness stand.

"So how long have you been a vocalist?" Daniels asked, immediately realizing that had indeed used his attorney tone after all.

The long, lanky singer with the greasy and thinning long blond hair smiled and quickly responded with a laugh: "Hell, I don't think I've ever been a vocalist. I just belt out songs I love. If your band plays loud enough, it drowns the singer out anyway. People in clubs love bands that rock, and if the singer doesn't screw up too much, they're happy."

The singer soothed his tonsils by taking a long gulp from his bottle of Budweiser.

"Why do you ask?"

Daniels felt as awkward as a clumsy pre-teen with his shoes tied together at his first school dance.

He paused for a couple minutes and replied: "Well, I've been singing rock classics since they were fresh releases and I thought it might be fun to try this ... even though I'm not a kid anymore."

"Well," said the Pigs of Deception vocalist, "go for it. But you need to dress down a bit. You look like an accountant or something."

"Actually a lawyer," grinned back Daniels.

"Solicitor, I got a good stage name for you -- Esquire!"

His yellow teeth beamed (if yellow can actually beam in a dark bar) back at Jack, who merely smiled.

"Listen, give me your business card, counselor. I know a lot of guys in bands around Miller County and if I hear of an opening, I'll let you know. You pretty much cover the usual bands -- the Stones, Zeppelin, the Animals, Clapton, Springsteen, Hendrix, The Doors, Van Halen?"

"Exactly," Daniels said, brightening. "I'm partial to The Doors. Some people think I sound a little like Morrison."

"No shit," said the singer. "Hell, we gotta a few Doors songs coming up in the next set -- *Light My Fire*, *Hello I Love You* and *L.A. Woman*. Why don't you step up to the mic and fill in for me? My Morrison ain't all that hot."

Daniels tried not to gulp. "Dressed like this?" he protested.

"Screw it," the singer snapped. "You're on. You might even get some clients out of this."

"Why, are they going to riot and get arrested for tearing down the place in protest?" Daniels asked, not feeling all that funny.

In fact, Daniels quickly began scanning the club to see if he recognized anybody. To his relief, he did not. Nevertheless, he hadn't felt this nervous since he had taken the bar exam. And at least he didn't have to do that before a live audience. He scrambled to the bar for another Jack Daniels to drown out any stage fright. But even before he took another shot of Jack, the steel in his spine stiffened and he realized that if he was going to become a rock vocalist, to paraphrase The Chamber Brothers, the time had come today (or rather tonight). So when it was time to take the stage a few minutes hence, the freshly minted Jack Daniels had his game, uh, stage face on.

The Pigs of Deception vocalist, Butch Braxton (who was not the town's founding father), bellowed into the microphone: "Boys and girls, this is a special moment in time. Here, for the very first time, is Pigs of Deception guest vocalist Jack Daniels. And that, believe it or not, IS his real name. And he's going to wail some Doors' songs in his best Jim Morrison!"

Then as the Pigs of Deception went right into *Light My Fire* as Daniels, a jolt of excitement and confidence shooting up and down his spinal cord like a manic elevator, walked up to Braxton and took the microphone from him.

From the first note Daniels exuded a commanding presence and was drop-your-beer-bottle good.

Without missing a beat, Daniels' rich baritone suddenly captivated everybody there, with the band playing with an extra dollop or two of adrenaline as Daniels compellingly brought the lyrics and Jim Morrison back to life. Who knew that an impersonator could bring back the dead and even throw in a funny encore?

Girl, bring along plenty of matches
It's gonna take a lot to ignite my fire
Grab a blowtorch too
But try not to set me on fire

By the time his revised *Light My Fire* had flickered out, a flame of applause shot through Blind Hermit's Tavern and Butch Braxton suddenly felt like Wally Pipp to Daniels' Lou Gehrig, who wound up playing a billion and two games at first base for the New York Yankees in the Babe Ruth era after Pipp missed a game with a hamstring or something twanged like a bad guitar string. Braxton was walking over to take the microphone from Daniels when the Pigs of Deception got right into *Hello I Love You* because everybody in Blind Hermit's could plainly hear that Jack Daniels was a Morrison sound-alike and a kickass rock and roll singer. Daniels practically stiff-armed Braxton and kept possession of the mic as if it were a ticket to ride to the future, with the here and now of the moment offering a delicious bit of foreshadowing.

The rocking crowd knew Jack Daniels' name and it loved him.

After the Pigs of Deception and Jack had belted out *L.A. Woman* with an electric sizzle, Daniels bowed and basked in the warmth of the patrons. The surge of excitement coursing through Jack was something he had never felt this intensely, even when he had won his first first-degree murder case. Daniels handed the mic back to an ashen Butch Braxton and bounded over to the bar for another Jack Daniels on the rocks. While at the bar, Daniels further bathed in adulation as guys and girls clapped him on the back, asking if he had ever sung on stage before.

"Never?" yelped one balding guy. "You gotta be shitting me!"

After exchanging in some excited talk with some others, a distinguished-looking guy in his 30s approached Jack -- which prompted Daniels to spin through his Rolodex of memories, trying to place the man's face.

"You probably don't remember me," said the thin man with impeccably combed blond hair. "Ryan Hartwell. I was a young assistant DA when you kicked my ass in the Benson-Davis rape trial. That son of a bitch was guilty as hell, and you got him off because I was no match for you. But I learned a lot from you and it helps me as a civil litigator these days. And now I find out that you also kick ass as a rock singer. Do you walk on water, too?"

Daniels looked uncomfortable even though his smile had not turned upside down.

"I was hoping nobody from my legal world would see or hear this," Jack said. "First time I've ever done this but always wanted to."

"You should have done it a long time ago," Hartwell gushed. "You're damn good. But I guess singing in local bars hardly pays what you bring in as an attorney."

"Hardly," Daniels laughed. "But this isn't about the money. It's about me. Thanks for the kind words. Let me buy you a drink. What are you having?"

"I mostly drink white wine, but let me toast you with Jack Daniels. On the rocks."

After the Pigs of Deception had finished their set, the band members all came over to Daniels and offered their congratulations.

"You kicked ass," said the guitarist, whose eyelids were so droopy he looked as if he was perpetually asleep. "If Butch here ever gets a sore throat, we now know we have a backup vocalist."

"Butch looks like a guy who just swallowed his microphone," cracked the towering bassist, putting a playful headlock on Braxton.

"Relax, Butch," laughed Daniels, "I'm not after your gig. You gave me a shot, and I owe you. If you ever need pro bono legal advice, just call me."

"You can handle my next divorce," Braxton quipped, looking relieved. "And keep rocking. I'll let you know if I hear of any local bands in need of a vocalist."

"I'm damn glad I came out tonight," Daniels beamed, buying a round for the band.

Looking at all the impressed faces surrounding him like a thicket of thirsty trees, Daniels knew his stage debut hardly had been like an ice pick in their ear drums.

Chapter 3

Jack Daniels was back to being John Daniels the following morning as he sat working on his office PC. Or so he thought. Because his alter ego Jack surfaced when his receptionist walked in giggling.

"How was your evening last night, John?" asked Susan, a perky and petite bundle of blonde energy in her late 40s. "Or should I call you Jack?"

Daniels groaned loud enough to be both John and Jack.

"OK, who do you know who was at Blind Hermit's Tavern?" he asked with a pained expression. "Or do I really want to know?"

"My niece Monica," replied Susan, smiling more broadly than a Jack O' Lantern pumpkin. "Actually, she said you were quite good. But you were dressed like a lawyer who had misplaced his suit and tie."

"Well, at least she didn't say I sucked," Daniels said.

"So what's up with the rock singer bit?" asked Susan, cutting to the chase.

"Always wanted to try it and I figured I'd better do it before they had to wheel me on stage," Daniels said, a sheepish grin hanging from his lips.

"Rockers are getting older all the time," Susan said. "Look at the Stones and The Who."

"Do you think if I started doing this regularly in local clubs that it would hurt my credibility?" Daniels asked, a storm cloud of concern trespassing across his forehead.

"Well, sort of," Susan said. "Then again, maybe not. Having a hobby doesn't have to marginalize your reputation as a defense attorney. If you're good in court and have the name, and you have both, that should be enough. After all, there have been very successful attorneys who are womanizers or drunks. Or spend a lot of time golfing. The difference here is the degree of exposure. A lot of people around here know you and the transition from John Daniels to Jack Daniels could be startling to some."

"I know," Daniels said, fingering the knot in his tie as if it were a Fender guitar. "I know."

"Then again, some of our clients won't care ... they're not exactly CEO types," Susan said with a laugh. "Why don't you give this a shot and see how it plays out?"

"You know, I just might," Daniels said, flashing a raffish grin. "If I can be cocksure in the courtroom and on stage perhaps that will just add to the Daniels mystique. After all, I am a Gemini."

"Get over yourself," she cracked. "You have some briefs to read. So rock out with those and rock on later."

"Your niece just had to be at Blind Hermit's, didn't she?"

"So glad she was."

Later that day Daniels was at a murder arraignment for a local beauty salon owner accused of drowning his wife in the bathtub when one of the sheriff deputies, a forty something country dude who spent most of his time pub crawling, busting balls and soothing his itchy trigger finger at shooting ranges when he wasn't serving warrants and falling asleep in his van because of his nocturnal hobbies, asked Daniels if he sang any rock standards done by bands other than The Doors.

"Was the whole damn town at Blind Hermit's last night?" quipped Daniels, trying to make light of something that suddenly felt heavy in his chest.

"Hell, I don't know," replied the deputy. "When I saw you up there impersonating Morrison, I lost sight of everybody else. I couldn't believe the honorable John Daniels was on stage.

Before you started singing, I was tempted to shoot you and put you of your misery."

Esteemed criminal defense attorney John Daniels dissed by a lazy deputy sheriff with a heart shaped like a revolver, thought the esteemed John Daniels. Or did the deputy merely throw Jack Daniels under the bus, wondered the newbie rock singer Jack Daniels.

John Daniels and Jack Daniels ... with apologies to Rudyard Kipling, Daniels (not sure if it was John or Jack or a combination of both) started whispering "never the twain shall meet" under his breath.

"Then you started singing and man, you were good, I ain't kidding you," the deputy sheriff continued. "I've seen you in the courtroom and I never thought you could be that cool. You were as cool as the underside of a pillow."

"Well, glad I didn't come across as some dork," Daniels said, somewhat relieved.

"Of course, it shocked the hell out of me," the deputy sheriff said, then offered some advice: "Maybe you should sing your closing arguments from now on."

"Yeah, like that's going to happen," Daniels said, ending the conversation.

For the remainder of the arraignment, Daniels felt out of sync -- sort of, pardon the pun, off key.

And it disturbed him. He obviously had to seriously consider whether he was going to continue to give voice to Jack Daniels.

Chapter 4

John Daniels, going out of his way not to be Jack Daniels by still wearing a suit and tie and looking grossly overdressed when he finally got to the Beer Bucket for a Friday night gig by the Rocking Pennsylvania Dutchmen, sat at a corner table in the back. He was absorbing the scene and the sound and just knowing he could sing the vocal cords off the Rocking Pennsylvania Dutchmen's lead crooner, Shoo Fly Pie. Of course, Daniels knew a guy going by Shoo Fly Pie couldn't be any sillier than a singer named Meat Loaf. Except Meat Loaf had a taste for performing and Shoo Fly's voice sounded like screeching tires screaming over broken glass.

Daniels was feeling the vibe of performing and thinking even if his credibility as an attorney suffered a bit, he had more money than he needed and could weather any loss of income. As he sipped on his Jack Daniels in lieu of Scotch, he just knew that the bottom line in certain things belonged just there -- at the bottom. He was thinking John could be John when needed and Jack could be Jack when needed.

He regretted wearing the suit a few minutes later when a hustling waitress slipped on a wet spot on the floor, lost her balance and dumped a whole pitcher of beer in his lap.

"Oh, shit!" she screamed, scrambling to her feet while Daniels' crotch wallowed in wetness and his penis cowered from the cold beer. Suddenly Daniels thought about dropping the whole rock singer charade. After all, the spores of unrest are typically nurtured in dark and dank places.

That feeling was fleeting.

Daniels obviously had been startled, but quickly recovered his poise.

"Well at least it's a dark suit," he laughed. "If it were a tan suit, it sure would look like I pissed my pants."

"I am so, so sorry," said the flustered waitress, who was as skinny as a 7-iron and didn't look a day over 12. "Can I pay for the dry cleaning?"

"Nah, that's OK," Daniels said kindly. "A bunch of napkins would be just fine."

The waitress set a world land speed record for a sprinting waitress through a crowded club to fetch and return with a stack of napkins.

"Thanks," replied Daniels, whose groin area felt like Ice Station Zebra.

"I wish I had my blow dryer handy," said the waitress, trying to defuse his discomfort. She flashed a weak smile.

"Yeah, I'm sure that would have everybody howling with laughter," he said. "Instead, please get me another Jack Daniels."

He handed her a 20-dollar bill and told her to keep the change.

"You are a nice guy," she said. "What are you doing here?"

"Why, is the place usually full of just bad guys?"

"You know what I mean. Guys can be such assholes. But you're different. You look like a CEO or something. We usually get working guys."

"Believe it or not, CEOs sometimes work," he quipped behind a grin. "It's hard work carrying all those big bonus checks to the bank."

She laughed and Jack saw how pretty she was ... if you liked 12-year-olds.

"So you ARE a CEO," she exclaimed.

"No, just a lawyer."

"What kind?"

"I keep bad guys out of jail. So they can come here and give you big tips."

"I think you defended all the lousy tippers," she laughed.

"I'm also thinking about becoming a rock singer. Would love to perform here some night."

The waitress looked as if she had just swallowed a carp.

"You are? You would?"

"Now don't run off and tell the manager just yet," Jack laughed. "I don't even have a band yet."

"I'd come hear you," she said. "Some of my favorite rock singers are old."

Suddenly her face colored crimson and she stammered: "Not that you are old."

"Yes, I am," Jack smiled. "You know you just might hear me sing here some night. I'll get to work on it."

"Cool," she said. "Let me go get your Jack. By the way, what's your name?"

"Jack. Jack Daniels."

"You're putting me on!"

"God's honest truth."

"You know, be Jack Daniels and the Shots! That rocks!"

"I'll drink to that," Jack laughed.

Daniels, more Jack than John at the moment as he sat sipping his Jack and listening to Shoo Fly Pie's mangled vocal cords mangle the patrons' hearing, just knew he could dabble as a rocker without rocking his legal career to any significant degree.

When the bassist in the Rocking Pennsylvania Dutchmen walked by his table on the way to the men's room, Daniels struck up a conversation with him and told him of his aspirations, being sure to mention that some people think he sounds like Jim Morrison.

"Dude, you look pretty straight to me to be a rock singer," commented the beer-bellied bassist with a gray beard and brown hair. "Let your hair grow a bit and find some crummy clothes. I wish we could dump Shoo Fly Pie but he's married to my sister and that would make for awkward Thanksgiving dinners."

"Dropping Shoo Fly Pie would be a marketing disaster for the Rocking Pennsylvania Dutchmen," Daniels cracked.

"You got that right. Just wish the man had been born with a set of pipes that weren't corroded. By the way, if you're serious about this, man, I know a local band that is looking for a new lead singer. They cover mostly classic rock, and it could be a good fit for you since you told me that's what you prefer. I know they do some Doors and if you do sound somewhat like Jim Morrison, well, there you go."

"That's great," Daniels said, the excitement playing loudly in his eyes. "What's the name of the band?"

"A kickass name," bellowed the bassist. "Coffeemate."

"Coffeemate?" asked Daniels, the confusion apparent on his face.

"Don't you get it? It's a knockoff on Cream. They like to do some British blues rock that Eric Clapton, Ginger Baker and Jack Bruce did. Their covers of *Crossroads, Spoonful, Born Under a Bad Sign, Strange Brew and Sunshine of Your Love* can be righteous."

"So how do I get in touch with them?"

"The lead guitarist is the band leader, a guy name Toad. But his real name is Bernie Silverstein. Give me your business card and I will email his phone number to you."

After glancing at the business card Daniels handed him, the bassist almost spilled his big gut laughing.

"John Daniels, the freaking defense attorney? Man, I've heard of you! You got my cousin off for armed robbery several years ago. Do you remember Lee Wentzel? I'm Bob Wentzel."

"The name Lee Wentzel does ring a bell," Daniels said. "How's he doing?"

"He's unemployed, but at least he stopped beating his old lady."

"That's good."

"Yeah, she finally left him."

"Oh."

"Listen, I won't tell Toad who you are, in case that freaks him out. I don't think he has any criminals in his family, so he may not recognize your name. Let him hear you sing first before he finds out. I'll just tell him I bumped into a guy who claims he can sing. Leave it up to him to follow up."

"Tell you what, you can tell him my name. Just say my name is Jack Daniels."

"Hey, that's righteous, brother. When you audition for Toad you need to give him a bout with pneumonia. Take his damn breath away."

Chapter 5

Bob Wentzel was notorious for not dotting his i's and crossing his t's but he plucked the right strings in his memory banks and did follow up by emailing Daniels Toad's phone number.

Daniels was excited when he got the email. But he did dawdle a bit in giving Toad a call. Daniels was nervous and indecisive, something he never was in the legal arena. In the legal realm, he felt like a warrior. In the rock realm, he felt like a schmuck. A too-buttoned-down schmuck. A too-buttoned-down, too-old schmuck. Besides, he was uncertain whether to call Toad Bernie Silverstein or Toad.

Daniels found procrastination to be a kidney crusher so he picked up his smartphone.

"What the hell am I doing?" John Daniels asked himself as he punched Toad's number.

"Going for it," answered Jack Daniels a beat later.

"Who you?" croaked Toad when he answered the phone.

"Toad?" Daniels replied.

"I'm Toad. There can't be two Toads," snapped Toad.

"I'm not Toad, I'm Jack Daniels."

"Pals with Jim Beam?"

Toad's belly laughs were a good indication he thought himself quite the humorist.

"And Johnnie Walker," retorted Daniels.

"What can I do for you?" asked Toad. "Pour you a shot?"

"Bob Wentzel gave me your name and number. Said you might be interested in a vocalist."

"Can you sing a lick?"

"More than a lick," Daniels said with a swagger in his voice.

"Whatta you sing?"

"Mostly classic rock. The Stones, Zeppelin, Clapton, Cream, The Animals, Clapton, Springsteen, Van Halen, The Doors, some others. I'm partial to The Doors because I sound a lot like Jim Morrison."

"What bands have you been in?"

Daniels cleared his throat to buy time for a moment or two.

"Uh, none," he answered, his voice dipping an octave.

"Huh? Did you say none?"

"Uh, yes," said Daniels, suddenly squirming like one of his victims on the witness stand.

"How old are you?"

"Well, I'm at the perfect age because I was in my prime when these classic rock bands were in their prime," responded Daniels, recovering his composure.

"Your age?" asked Toad, losing interest.

"Uh, 57."

"Do you look it?"

Toad would have made a good prosecutor, Daniels thought.

"Not at all," Daniels said.

"Sing some of *Light My Fire* for me," Toad barked, putting Daniels' feet to the fire.

Daniels thought a phone audition without instrumental accompaniment was likely career suicide and wondered why this particular song usually was requested when he told somebody he sounded like Morrison.

But it was now or never, so Daniels envisioned himself in a club and morphed into the closest thing to Morrison you'll hear on earth while listening on a phone with no instrumental accompaniment:

You know that it would be untrue
You know that I would be a liar
If I was to say to you

Girl, we couldn't get much higher
Come on baby, light my fire
Come on baby, light my fire
Try to set the night on fire

The time to hesitate is through
No time to wallow in the mire
Try now we can only lose
And our love become a funeral pyre
Come on baby, light my fire
Come on baby, light my fire
Try to set the night on fire, yeah

When he was done singing, the other end was silent for a mere hiccup or two. Toad was floored by how luminescent Daniels' voice was.

"Damn, that was sweet," Toad said, sincerity coating his tongue. "You do sound like Morrison! We're practicing next Tuesday night at 6 in my garage. Can you make that?"

"Hell, yes!" replied Daniels.

The rush Jack Daniels felt at that precise moment was almost as good as sex. Almost, mind you.

"You could be the spoon that stirs Coffeemate!" croaked Toad.

"I'll drink to that!" Daniels laughed. "Of course, Jack Daniels and Coffeemate make for a sickening blend strictly from a beverage perspective."

"Hell, it ain't about that," Toad shouted. "It's all about the music."

Speaking of music, Jack Daniels became John Daniels again moments after hanging up with Toad. It was then that it hit him like a grand piano dropping 17 floors from a studio window that he had a murder trial scheduled the following week. Murder trials, pardon the pun, are real killers when it comes to a defense attorney's schedule and Daniels realized he had about as much chance of making that band practice as he did singing opera at the Met. During trials, especially murder trials, he had an extreme narrowing of focus -- like sighting down a rifle barrel. He was totally myopic.

For a fleeting moment he thought about calling Toad to tell him he couldn't make it. Then he decided his life was as important as the life of the 18-year-old he was trying to save for allegedly killing a 36-year-old father of six in a barber shop robbery. While innocent until proven guilty and while Daniels would move heaven and earth, not to mention purgatory just in case it still existed, to defend the boy, he wasn't going to sacrifice his Tuesday night rock gig to keep the kid's guilty ass out of prison for life.

When the ensuing Tuesday evening rolled around and John Daniels had gone through jury selection and opening statements in the murder trial, Jack Daniels was racing to make band practice, still in his $2,000 three-piece suit that was crisper than fresh potato chips.

When he walked up to the worn, semi-detached two-story home in a working class neighborhood, Daniels realized that as a rock vocalist at the moment he looked as out of place as the village idiot at a Mensa convention. He had meant to change but once the judge had excused them for the day, there simply had been no time. So instead of dressing like a grungy rocker, he looked like the president of a local glee club.

When Toad answered the door, Jack knew why he had been nicknamed that. Toad had a stubby body with short legs and warty, dry skin. If the guy had any groupies, they had to be blind with no sense of touch.

Toad, of course, was equally taken aback at what he saw.

"Just leave your day job?" Toad croaked. "Are you a funeral director or something?"

"Nah, just ran out of my good clothes and had nothing else to wear today," Daniels retorted, trying to keep his true identity quiet for now even though his suit screamed professional as loudly as a wailing guitar with an amp on steroids.

"Well, unloosen your tie and meet the rest of the band."

Toad, who perpetually wore the pained expression of a guy watching his Jaguar catch fire in the driveway even though he drove an ancient Jeep that spewed parts, escorted Daniels through the dimly lit home with cheap furniture and down into the unfinished basement, where the band practiced on cement next to the gas furnace and gas water heater. Daniels couldn't help but notice some cobwebs hanging from the overhead pipes.

The Coffeemate band mates couldn't help but notice that Daniels looked straighter than 6 o'clock, so square he looked divisible by four. And he couldn't help but notice that they were hardly a handsome cast of characters. When someone first mentioned that beauty is only skin deep but ugly goes down to the bone, he must have been at a Coffeemate gig.

Besides Toad on lead guitar, the band members -- drum roll, please -- were:

Bones McKinney on bass -- a 6-foot, 6-inch crew cut string bean in his early 30s who was all gawky angles and intersections with a heavily freckled face, no chin, an Adam's Apple bigger than a Grand Canyon boulder and a cowlick that wouldn't quit even if you staked it out in the sun. While not exactly bad to the bone, he believed that being bad was better than being good because while the good sleep better, the bad enjoy the waking hours much more.

Pudge Klumpf on drums -- a chrome-domed, 328-pound bear of a man in his late 30s who had pierced ears, eyebrows and nose (which was enormous) and arms absolutely polluted with tattoos. He also had an unlit cigar stuck in his mouth. His ample stature gave credence to the theory that bulldozer beats tulip. If he went swimming in Loch Ness, the monster would get out. He was so big he wasn't born, he was founded. Pudge claimed he injected moose testosterone and once dressed in Vera Wang on stage to win a $3,000 bet.

Ziggy Zmroczek on rhythm guitar -- a short, nervous, pale mouse of a man in his late 40s who had long thinning hair but still enough left to manage a scraggly ponytail and who blinked more frequently than an airport tower. Before he fell from grace because of a rampant masturbation hobby, he once aspired to be pro-am partners with Jesus even though neither the Son of God nor Ziggy played golf.

After the round of introductions, Daniels flashed a grin and quipped: "Toad, Bones, Pudge and Ziggy. I guess you needed a guy with a plain name. I'm Jack. Jack Daniels."

"Yup, that's a classic," squeaked Bones, whose vocal cords evidently were as gawky as the rest of him.

"You don't look like no rocker to me," Pudge growled. "Grow your hair. Get some tats. But first let's hear what you got. If you can bring it, I don't give a damn what you look like. Hell, you could look like my mother's minister for all I care."

Daniels hadn't been to confession since he grew weary of telling the priest how many times he had masturbated in the past month when he was 13, but he realized now was the time to hit the confession box.

"Well, I hope I pass the audition," grinned Daniels, "but no way in hell am I getting tattoos. It would screw with my day job. I'm a criminal defense attorney. So if you ever kill a guy, call me. I'll give you a 10 percent discount. The offer stands for all of you."

"I'll be damned," piped up Ziggy. "I knew I recognized you. I've seen you in the paper and on television. You're a big-time lawyer. Why you messing with this?"

"The dude loves to sing, and he has the chops," Toad said. "He did a helluva job with *Light My Fire* on the phone. I can't wait to hear him sing with us backing him up."

So, without further ado, they got down to it ... Jack playing the part of Jim Morrison ... Coffeemate playing the part of The Doors ... they rocked and rolled through a whole medley of Doors' classics ... *Light My Fire, Alabama Song, Hello I Love You, L.A. Woman, The End, Soul Kitchen, End Of The Night, Love Her Madly, Love Me Two Times* and *Riders On The Storm*.

While he was belting out the lyrics, Jack Daniels could sense the whole band was digging him -- his voice and his style. He looked straight but he sang and moved with a silky, sexy, smoldering presence. They went from song to song, with no conversation at all.

When The Doors' session concluded, Pudge piped up: "This is awesome. But we can't just be a Doors' cover band. What about all the other material we play?"

"I sound like Morrison, but I love singing all the rock classics," Daniels replied. "So not a problem. I don't want to just do Doors either."

"I think we got ourselves a helluva vocalist," Ziggy said.

"Amen, brother!" gushed Bones.

"A done deal," Toad said, exchanging high fives with Daniels.

"Not yet," Daniels said. "Let's do a quick medley of non-Doors material to convince you bastards I can sing whatever I need to sing!"

"Let's rock, brother!" Pudge roared.

And then Daniels stirred Coffeemate through a rousing set of *Satisfaction* by the Stones, *House of the Rising Sun* by The Animals, *Runnin' With the Devil* by Van Halen, *Born To Run* by Springsteen, *Every Breath You Take* by Sting, *Stairway to Heaven* by Zeppelin, *Go Now* by the Moody Blues, *Sexual Healing* by Marvin Gaye, *Twist & Shout* by The Beatles, and a medley of Cream songs ... *Strange Brew*, *Tales of Brave Ulysses* and *Toad* (from whence Bernie Silverstein got his nickname).

Daniels, while still sounding a lot like Jim Morrison, nailed every one of them and then some.

"I think you passed the audition," Toad said, beaming dimples he didn't have.

Adrenaline, excitement and satisfaction geysered throughout Daniels' nervous system like a speedball on crack. He had never felt such a rush. At least not with his shoes on.

But his euphoria was fleeting. He had to bid his new band mates a quick goodbye because he had a murder trial stalking him like a timber wolf and he would be up half the night prepping for the next day's courtroom theatrics and fireworks. He had an 18-year-old boy who deserved his attention.

He wound up being up almost all night and morning. John Daniels the attorney was more anal than a colonoscopy. He embraced details with gusto, even if they were as prickly as an ulcerous porcupine. His zeal for homework had served him well in school, college, law school and in his legal practice. For a guy who had been a half-assed Boy Scout whose sum total of merit badges was zero, he always was prepared. But he wasn't this time. His dalliance with Jack Daniels the rock singer had imperiled this murder trial and in the wee hours the guilt gnawed on him like a bear just out of hibernation gnawing on ribs. He realized the gulf between John Daniels and Jack Daniels was oceanic.

Chapter 6

Eddie Rodriguez was cockier than a rooster in a henhouse and totally had a disconnect with reality. He was on trial for killing Lou DeMario, a barber who worked 70 hours a week in his one-chair Braxton shop to support his wife and six kids. Eddie was a product of the mean Braxton streets. He was such a street dude it was surprising that he wasn't dressed in asphalt. Even in the cheap suit Daniels bought him for the trial, Eddie Rodriguez didn't clean up well.

He was a nasty cockroach of a human being who belonged to the south end of a bull walking north.

Eddie seemed more concerned what the word on the street was than what his fate was going to be. Two eyewitnesses saw him fleeing DeMario's shop after gunshots shattered what little serenity the neighborhood had. They shouted at a passing police car and Rodriguez, after tripping over the shoestrings of his unlaced sneaker, was easy to apprehend.

The cops charged him with second-degree murder, claiming Eddie didn't enter the shop with a premeditated intent of killing the barber. It was only when Lou DeMario had swung a baseball bat at Eddie after having a gun pulled on him that Eddie pulled the trigger. The cops said DeMario died instantly, plopping in a pile of hair and that Eddie took the whopping total of $47.34 from the cash register.

Eddie had proclaimed his innocence ever since his arrest, but the case seemed cut and dried. His prints were on the murder weapon and the two eyewitnesses had known him since he was a little kid. Daniels was convinced the kid was guilty and had unsuccessfully tried to talk him into pleading guilty, hoping for a reduced sentence. But Eddie steadfastly refused, insisting he was as innocent as a 13-year-old girl. Of course, there were girls in Braxton who had their first baby by the time they were 13.

A bone-tired Daniels was off his game just a bit in the courtroom the day after his rousing audition with Coffeemate. His lack of preparation bothered him as he conducted his cross of one of the two eyewitnesses in his sleep.

A lady in her 60s was an unwitting contributor to his somewhat impaired self-assurance by being dumber than a porch stoop.

"How do you know Eddie Rodriguez?" he asked Martha Jones, whose 200-plus pounds were poured into a yellow dress that was straining to keep its seams from imploding.

"I knew his mom because we both went to Dr. Pike. Eddie's mom had had several of her children by Dr. Pike and said he was really good."

After that malapropism, the judge almost split his gavel trying to restore order in the courtroom.

Eddie didn't help matters by leaping to his feet and shouting, "My mom was no whore!"

The judge, a 75-year-old senior judge named Gomer Smith who was stern enough to be named John Calvin, admonished Daniels to keep his client in line or he would be held in contempt of court.

Daniels whispered in Eddie's ear to shut the hell up.

"OK, man. But she be talking bad about my momma," Eddie snapped.

Mrs. Jones sat there aghast in silence, totally oblivious to what she had said to trigger the outburst.

Meanwhile, retiring from the law and rocking on was appealing to Jack Daniels, making his first appearance in a courtroom. But enough of John Daniels remained in the courtroom to adroitly find inconsistencies in Mrs. Jones' eyewitness account.

John Daniels wasn't happy with Jack Daniels when the second eyewitness, a 65-year-old pastor with a deep voice that sounded like the voice of God, blurted out before Daniels could even ask his first question, "Aren't you the guy who does a mean Jim Morrison?"

That, of course, elicited another round of laughter and prompted the judge to put his gavel back to work in silencing the courtroom.

Daniels was stunned and angry with himself for a moment for being stupid enough to pursue his rock dream while being a high-profile attorney. But he hadn't become a high-profile attorney by not being good on his feet.

Daniels immediately relaxed, smiled broadly and replied to the thin pastor, who remained smiling.

"I admire a man of the cloth who knows there is good music outside of hymns," Daniels said. "And yes, I've been known to do a fair impersonation of Jim Morrison. Which does nothing to help me in my day job, obviously. But you, sir, if I may so respectfully say, do a righteous impersonation of the voice of God with your baritone. That must be a great help to you in your day job."

That, too, drew loud laughter and Judge Smith was radish red with anger and his right forearm was getting sore from pounding the gavel.

"Mr. Daniels, one more outburst and I will hold you and your client in contempt of court!" the judge bellowed.

"Understood," replied Daniels, calmly.

Daniels then had the pastor eating out of his hand as if there were Hershey Kisses cupped on his palm and the Rev. Solomon Graybill was no match for a savvy attorney like Daniels. John poked enough holes in the pastor's aged memory to cast some doubt on whether he had actually had seen Eddie Rodriguez or just somebody else who looked like him.

Bottom line, Daniels, both the John and Jack versions, was a born performer. Whether he was addressing the jury or crooning to an audience, he was a gifted communicator who could move people.

In his closing argument trying to save Eddie Rodriguez's guilty ass, Daniels sounded like a galvanic preacher to whom the birds would listen. In contrast, the short, skinny assistant district attorney trying the case was as stoic as a statue shaped by a medieval sculptor. In the end, only because Daniels had cast so much doubt on the credibility of the eyewitnesses and preying on a predominantly white jury that thought all Hispanics looked alike, a miracle broke a sweat and Eddie Rodriguez was found not guilty.

The murder victim's widow and kids were awash in anger and tears. The *Braxton Bugle* and WBRA-TV reported the verdict as though it had been a miscarriage of justice, implying that John Daniels was just too damn slick for the scales of justice to be balanced. He had proven yet again that legends are great for the long haul.

John Daniels was pleased with his professional performance; displeased that a killer was walking the streets. But it was his job and he grudgingly accepted it. But he also knew that if he saved his money, there was a much better -- if much less lucrative -- gig out there for him as a rock singer.

Daniels was a Gemini. And he had two faces. Despite the verdict, John Daniels' face was wearing an upside down smile. Jack Daniels' face was wearing a smile that was sunny side up.

Chapter 7

The Arizona Bar and Grill was so jammed the sardines impersonating booze-drinking men and women could have used crowbars to create elbow room. Of course, these sardines came with elbows.

It was too hot for coffee but not for Coffeemate.

And matters got even hotter when the crowd really began digging Coffeemate's new vocalist.

Jack Daniels' vocal cords were amped for his Coffeemate debut and his voice never sounded more Morrison-like. Wearing all black, he looked sleek and dangerous. More importantly, he sounded sleek and dangerous. With generous dollops of sexuality thrown in.

For a moment on stage he paused between songs and marveled at the delicious hubris of it all.

Jack, Toad on the lead guitar, Ziggy Zmroczek on rhythm guitar, Bones McKinney on bass and Pudge Klumpf on drums were a cover band that sounded like The Doors and *were* The Doors if you closed your eyes.

And they also rocked on righteously when doing Cream, the Stones, The Animals, Springsteen, Van Halen, etc.

After the last set when Coffeemate and everybody else was drenched in satisfying sweat, the Coffeemate band mates sat at the bar to soak in a few beers and all the adulation.

And one particular relatively young lady in her early 30s seemed to really groove on Jack Daniels. A striking, long-legged blonde, Ashley Dupree was a free-spirited hair stylist and sometimes cosmetic counter sales lady enjoying a night out on the town with her friend Chrissy Patton. However, Chrissy got a call that her 7-year-old daughter had an upset stomach and

Ashley, who was too into the Morrison clone to leave, opted to hang around and meet him.

Ashley, with skin as smooth as silk on satin, was not in the habit of hanging out to meet guys. Her life was the total inverse. Guys flocked to her like, well, groupies to rock stars. But Ashley never was a groupie, never needed to be and never wanted to be.

But she was an impulsive person and there was something about Jack Daniels ... his look ... his presence ... his whatever ... that had magnetized her and invisibly tethered her to the scene. And when Ashley Dupree made the scene, it always came with a refreshing splash.

While Jack was sitting on a bar stool sandwiched between Bones and Pudge, Ashley came up from behind Jack and poured some of her Perrier mineral water down the back of his shirt.

Daniels obviously couldn't have been more startled if somebody had jammed an air hose up his nose. He whirled around angrily while screaming, "What the hell!"

Until his anger instantly melted like ice cubes thrown into a blast furnace when his eyes gazed upon the comely Ashley Dupree.

"Nice mouth," shot back Ashley through her glistening pearly whites. "Relax, I was just messing with you!"

"Damn, the vocalists always get the ones who want to screw with them and screw them," Bones cracked.

The smile on Jack's face looked like it was parted by Moses.

"I take it you're a fan of Jim Morrison," he said, winking.

"Just say his voice always turned me on," Ashley said. "But that's not why I'm in your face. I like your face. And I want to know more about you. Like why is a prominent defense attorney lighting up the club scene? I thought it might be cool to get to know you."

"Well, just say you meet more interesting people in a bar than you do in a courtroom," Daniels retorted. "How did you know I'm a lawyer?"

"Several years ago you defended a friend of mine who owns a tattoo parlor. You remember Needles the Ink Man? You helped him beat an assault rap or something. He said you were a freaking genius. He offered you some free tats, but you declined. Foolish. Needles has inked me up a bit but only in relatively discreet spots. I'll have to show you sometime when I get to know you better. You could have gotten inked and still kept your day job."

"What's your day job? Your name would be nice as well."

"I'm a beauty stylist and also sell cosmetics. The name is Ashley. And your name is Daniels. But it's not Charlie, right?"

"Charlie Daniels it's not. But I do have a brother named Charlie, believe it or not. My name is John Daniels as an attorney; Jack Daniels as a singer; and just Daniels to my friends."

"Well, Jack works for me. Buy me a drink, Jack, and we'll talk about the criminal defense code and music. I play a little guitar and have done some backup vocals."

Daniels got off the barstool, took Ashley's hand, and confidently said, "Let's try to find a table and a waitress in this place. What are you drinking?"

"I don't know Jack so I'd love a shot of Jack Daniels," she purred.

"I think that can be arranged," Daniels replied, a rakish grin spreading over his lips.

Over some Jack Daniels on the rocks at a corner table, Ashley and Daniels soon realized that despite their differences in age, backgrounds and professional circles, they had a connection stout enough to hang drywall -- and a relationship -- on.

The next day Judge Nathan Hawthorne thought Daniels might be wearing some dirty laundry under his expensive suit when he saw him holding hands with Ashley as they walked into The Nut Bar Restaurant for lunch. But what caught the judge's attention more than the hand-holding was the outfit Ashley was wearing. She was sporting torn jeans, a short blouse that was equally facile at exposing chunks of her ample breasts, abs, lower back and a few of her tattoos.

After Daniels spotted the judge, he nervously mentioned to Ashley that the white-haired gentleman seated alone at a table was a Miller County judge.

Daniels was as paranoid as a getaway driver when he and Ashley approached Judge Hawthorne's table but Ashley felt no restraint. Before Daniels could even say hello, the impulsive Dupree plopped down on a chair at the judge's table and quipped, "Hope you don't mind if we join you for lunch, Judge!"

For an awkward moment that seemed frozen into a damned eternity, Daniels and Hawthorne couldn't have been more shocked if somebody had shot live voltage into their ears.

When the hot jolt had subsided, Daniels sat down as well while the judge licked his dentures to ensure they still were intact.

"This is Ashley, Nathan," Daniels said, more than a tad sheepish. "Ashley, this is Judge Hawthorne."

"I never saw a judge without his black robe before," Ashley said. "Hope we didn't screw up your lunch."

The judge, despite his 69 years and his 33 years on the bench, was not stiffer than Queen Elizabeth.

"I hate dining alone and when my wife stiffed me for lunch today, I was hoping somebody I knew would walk in. And now I realize that I don't know John as well as I did."

"The John I know is a Jack and he's a damn dead ringer for Jim Morrison, at least voice-wise," purred Ashley.

"Jack, huh?" replied the judge, arching his eyebrows and peering over his reading glasses at John/Jack. "Morrison? I must tell you I have to hear you sing sometime because I loved The Doors."

Daniels' eyebrows did jumping jacks from pure shock, since he had assumed that the judge would have as much interest in The Doors as a blind man would have in rainbows.

"Really?" asked Daniels, who couldn't have been more uncomfortable if somebody had turned his boxers into a tourniquet.

"Hell, I wasn't an old fart all my life," laughed the judge. "Where do you sing besides the shower, uh, Jack?"

"John's fine," Daniels said. "In local clubs. Jack Daniels sounds better for a rock vocalist."

"Rock vocalist? Who would have thought that? I'm impressed."

"You're kidding me," Daniels replied, smiling. "I've tried to keep my hobby as a singer separate from my legal practice."

"It's a small town, Jack, and if you're gonna sing in clubs around here, people are going to find out," Ashley interjected coyly.

"Especially when you are serving as my unpaid publicist," Jack retorted, laughing.

"I take it you two met at one of John's singing gigs?" the judge said to Ashley.

"I love The Doors and Morrison and when I heard Jack do some of their covers, well, he had me instantly. But just so you know, I'm not a groupie. Not one of those skanks."

"I didn't mean to imply that at all, young lady," said Judge Hawthorne. "And what is your profession."

"Beauty stylist mostly. While you get to sit down on your job, I'm on my feet all day."

"Very true," said the judge, chuckling. "And I don't have to make small talk."

"You have the gavel to shut them up," Ashley giggled.

"True. And I've slammed it down a few times when John's clients got carried away."

"Well, I'm not exactly representing altar boys all the time," Daniels said.

"Did you ever represent a pedophile priest, Jack?" asked Ashley, startling her new boyfriend even more than the judge.

"Uh, no," Jack said haltingly, discovering that Ashley's free-spirited nature wasn't always delightfully charming.

"Good! Because they're disgusting," pronounced Ashley.

"So Judge, don't you agree that the DA is doing a great job of clearing some of the backlog of criminal cases?" Daniels asked, quick to change the subject.

Ashley surprisingly got the hint and quickly excused herself to the ladies' room.

As soon as Ashley left the table, Daniels felt compelled to do some damage control.

"Nathan, I guess you think I'm going through a midlife crisis but I assure you that I am not. I truly have had a lifetime fascination with becoming a rock singer, at least on the local club level."

"Don't you think such an avocation could compromise your legal reputation? Perception can be a damaging thing."

"Yes, I am aware of that. But hopefully intelligent people can discern what is a hobby and what is not."

"As lovely as your lady friend is, does her attire at lunch say anything about your image in the community to you?"

"I see your point, but I love the contrast in us and relish our differences."

"You are an outstanding attorney and you have an impeccable reputation among your peers and I would hate to see that damaged," intoned the judge. "Still, one must be happy in their personal life. Perhaps being a rock singer as an after-hours hobby is not that big of a deal. And perhaps you can convince your girlfriend that a little fashion compromise on her part would be helpful to you."

"True. We'll see how this plays out but I will give your concerns due consideration. And I appreciate you being so candid with me. Meanwhile, you have to admit we certainly saved you from a dull lunch by yourself."

"Hardly dull at all, John. And let me know your upcoming appearances with your band. Maybe I will invite some other judges and lawyers along. That way you might be able to be the entertainment at the next bar association dinner. Word-of-mouth marketing still works in this age of social media."

"Spoken with the wisdom of Solomon, Nathan. No wonder you make such a good judge."

John Daniels tried to silently swallow his gulp. He was not successful.

Chapter 8

Daniels' toes were getting facile at navigating the tightrope he was walking, trying to balance the demands of his legal career with his burgeoning rock hobby. Not to mention finding time for the comely and never boring Ashley.

So John/Jack was enjoying the full throttle of satisfaction one Friday night as he and his alter ego, Jim Morrison, wowed a rowdy crowd at The Den, a rough-and-tumble bar in rural Miller County.

Light My Fire had just finished resonating from his throat when four cops busted in.

"What the hell?" a startled Daniels reflexively said into his microphone.

One of the cops rushed up to the stage and Daniels immediately recognized him as Luke Olsen, who had testified against a few of Daniels' clients.

"Sorry, John," said Olsen, a granite statue of a man with moving lips, "but we have to interrupt."

Olsen announced over the microphone that the district attorney's office was immediately shutting the joint down for being a nuisance bar.

"Bullshit!" yelled Pudge Klumpf, pounding on his drums for emphasis. Pudge hated anything disrupting the music, even if it was the strong arm of the law. His displeasure stirred the crowd like a straw in a cocktail.

Luke Olsen whirled faster than a top, or in this case a cop, and grabbed Pudge's shirt.

The patrons hushed for a moment, almost as if they suddenly found themselves at High Mass in a church. Then quickly became unruly. That quickly ended when the other three cops began working the crowd by brandishing but not using their nightsticks and Olsen commanded into the microphone, "Everybody out. Now! Or we will arrest you."

The crowd's courage shrank like Chippendales in a cold pool.

Olsen put down the mic and growled at Pudge, "Knock it off, pal, or I'll arrest you."

"Go ahead and my lawyer will get me off!" Pudge screamed, flexing his beer muscles. "Jack Daniels is my attorney and he is an eyewitness to your police brutality."

"Knock it the hell off, Pudge," snapped Daniels. "Shut up and be quiet. We're outta here, too. Let's pack up our equipment."

Pudge settled down and as the crowd left the bar, Coffeemate gathered its gear.

While doing so, the bar owner kept screaming at Olsen, disputing that his place had routinely been a haven for drug trafficking and underage drinking.

"Want to represent me?" the owner yelled over to Daniels.

"No thanks," Daniels quickly replied. "I'm not mixing my day job with my night job."

"You really need to be doing this?" Olsen asked Daniels.

"Sometimes I wonder," Daniels said.

"You should," said the cop.

Daniels still was wondering the next night when he picked up Ashley to accompany him to the annual Miller County Bar Association dinner.

She looked absolutely ravishing but she was showing a bit too much cleavage and her exposed back revealed her tattoo of Daffy Duck that sat just above her ass.

Daniels bit his lip because the rest of her looked good enough to munch on ... and that would have been much tastier than the rubber chicken being served at the dinner.

"You're looking mighty conservative in your pinstriped suit, sir," Ashley chirped. "By the way, I know you hate my dress. But I figured I'd loosen up the judicial system a bit tonight."

"Nah," cracked Daniels. "All the wives dress like that. And the husbands wear motorcycle jackets."

"Very funny," Ashley said, mussing his hair. "You know how I dress makes you hotter than a bowl of Texas chili. And tonight I'm gonna cook you like a chicken-fried steak."

"Sounds better than the rubber chicken we are going to have at the dinner," laughed Daniels.

"I'll just eat the dessert anyway," smiled Ashley. "Gotta keep my girlish figure."

When they arrived at the Corona Plaza Hotel, none of the other women seemed to have Daffy Duck tattooed on their ass but it wouldn't have mattered if they had. Because all eyes were on Ashley, both her ass and her chest. She, of course, could have cared less. While flamboyant and free-spirited, she was hardly narcissistic. Believe it or not. She was just too laid back to be that self-centered.

As Ashley and Daniels mingled during the reception hour, he noted that every lawyer and judge in the place seemed to be vying for his attention. And he knew they were only making small talk so they could get a closer look at Ashley's assets. Of course, Daniels did notice that some of their wives definitely were flashing disapproval and jealously in their glances.

Dutch Flanagan, who specialized in insurance subrogation (definitely not a sexy vocation), did manage to whisper to Daniels while threatening to spill his glass of red wine over both their suits, "Bet you're the first guy to leave the dinner tonight. Can't say that I blame you."

Inside, Daniels was not terribly worried that Ashley would be outlandish in her behavior at dinner. While she could show flashes of being an untamed filly at times, she was intelligent, sophisticated when she wanted to be, and somewhat mindful of his profession. A gathering of lawyers was not the same as a gathering of drunken fraternity brothers or rednecks high on Red Bull and red blood. And, for the most part, Ashley did fulfill Daniels' expectations ... if you overlooked her temporary loss of filter when Mrs. Hinnershitz burped during dinner.

Bertie Hinnershitz was married to Bert Hinnershitz, the managing general partner of Hinnershitz, Klusewitz, Abramowitz and Mazurkiewicz.

His firm was the most influential corporate law firm in Miller County and Bert and Bertie were very active in charitable causes. They were class acts. So when Bertie erupted with a belch at the table that also included Daniels and Ashley, it shocked everyone who heard it. All were stunned that Bertie did so in public and would have been thoroughly surprised to discover that she even burped in private.

Of course, Ashley had no frame of reference. So when Bertie's belch threatened to shatter all glass in that zip code, Ashley laughed uproariously while exclaiming, to the distress of the more sanctimonious and abstemious among them, "Holy shit! What the hell was hidden in your mashed potatoes?"

Bertie, already mortified beyond comprehension, was seriously considering jamming her dinner fork and salad fork into her eyes and stirring until she died. And that was *before* she heard Ashley's remark.

Bert Hinnershitz, wishing that he could cover Ashley in tuna oil and lower her into a tank full of barracuda, had to be restrained from throwing a big right hand at her but nobody could stop him from bellowing "Slimy slut!" at Ashley.

As for Daniels, he remained unflappable externally while internally he wanted to spank his girlfriend in a non-sexual way.

"Bert, please calm down," Daniels said calmly. "Ashley here meant no disrespect to Bertie. It was just that your wife's unfortunate belch shocked my girlfriend into temporary insanity."

Ashley, a smile plastered to her ruby-red lips in self-defense, quickly apologized to Mr. and Mrs. Hinnershitz, blaming too much wine for her temporary gaffe in etiquette.

"Besides, lady, burps sometimes just come out," Ashley said to Bertie. "It's not like you consciously were excavating your left nostril."

Before Bertie could perish from an instant stroke, Ashley then quickly flattered Bert and Bertie so smoothly that they didn't realize they were being played better than any of the instruments in Coffeemate gigs. No small feat considering that Bert's IQ must have had four figures and he was as cynical as a hanging judge in the Old West. Chalk it up to the power of charm and cleavage. Especially the cleavage in Bert's case.

By the time Ashley was done with the Hinnershitzes, she had booked Coffeemate to play at their next charity fundraiser for breast cancer awareness.

"A lady can't go wrong with pink," Bertie said in closing their conversation.

Daniels was so wired at this point he felt his pants zipper vibrating. And not because he was sporting a hard-on.

On the way home, the frost on Daniels' windshield had nothing to do with the weather.

"You're pissed, aren't you, hon?" Ashley asked sweetly.

"Knock off the crap, Ash," he said sourly. "I love you and I respect that we have different personalities and all. But damn it you know better than that. If you love me, you will have respect for me when we are socializing with my associates. If you love me, don't disrespect me or embarrass me. Rein yourself in when the circumstances and context dictate. You know that. You just need to dial back the impulsiveness. You need a damn filter."

"So you want me to change me because you are ashamed of me," Ashley said, beginning to sob.

"Don't play me and don't be a child!"

"Wanna spank me, daddy?"

"You are too much," he said, a smile softening his tone. "When we get home, light my fire and we'll move on."

"Consider it done," Ashley laughed while massaging her breasts.

"You want me to drive off the road?" Daniels asked.

The famed criminal defense attorney again fell victim to Ashley's charms, even though his better judgment knew, well, better. But man does not live by bread and brain alone. Frequently there has to be a beverage and a dick to give man life.

Chapter 9

Speaking of judgment, Ashley could have shown better judgment when two weeks later she impulsively knocked off work to watch Daniels in court during a murder trial.

As murder trials go, it was nothing notable in Miller County. Drug dealer kills another drug dealer. The accused, Pedro Gonzalez, had a rap sheet almost as long as the PA criminal code. And he was only 24. He allegedly shot Tino Martinez between the eyes one dark night at Seventh and Vine, a notorious red-light district in downtown Braxton. But the handgun was never found. Gonzalez was arrested for the crime because the lone eyewitness happened to be Albert Binkley, a Braxton police captain who was quite familiar with Gonzalez -- having arrested him twice for heroin trafficking.

Daniels wasn't going to take the case but Gonzalez's gay lover said he could meet his legal fees and claimed to be in bed with Gonzalez at the time of the shooting. And further claimed that Gonzalez's estranged identical twin brother, Tito, who was trying to muscle in on Pedro's drug turf, had killed Martinez. Jose Chacon, the gay lover, said he would testify that he was in bed with Gonzalez at the time of the murder. Pedro Gonzalez had told investigators about his twin, but they had scoffed at him.

The circumstances of the trial made it an instant media sensation in Braxton, Allentown and Philadelphia. Daniels' was working the trial masterfully until the afternoon Ashley strode into the courtroom, wearing a form-fitting pink dress that she somehow shoehorned herself into without busting a disc or two.

Suffice it to say, Daniels had been skeptical about whether Pedro Gonzalez and Chacon were indeed gay. And if they weren't, he gave them credit for their creativity and their balls.

Gays are not always thought highly of in the Latino drug-trafficking culture. Which is why Gonzalez and Chacon thought it was a great cover and alibi.

Well, without uttering a word, Ashley sort of screwed the pooch. Because both Pedro and Jose while on the witness stand couldn't take their eyes off Ashley. They did everything but foam at the mouth. Daniels naively hoped nobody in the courtroom actually noticed this because everybody -- including the judge and jury -- seemed to be doing the same. However, that was a thin reed for Daniels to lean his hopes on. And that reed snapped as if in a high wind when Chacon exclaimed a whistling "caramba" as he exited the witness stand, sending laser beams of sexual desire at the defense attorney's girlfriend sitting and oozing sultry. That got everybody's attention in the courtroom and at that precise moment Daniels knew a guilty verdict was as predictable as the morning sunrise.

"You're screwed," Daniels whispered to Gonzalez at the defense table. "What the hell is with Chacon?"

"I gotta hope the jury thinks he's bisexual," said Gonzalez, looking like he was going to puke.

"Dream on," Daniels said, disgusted with Chacon and livid with Ashley.

The closing arguments were the next day but Daniels realized that they were mere formalities now. The pooch indeed was screwed -- up the ass.

When Daniels got home that night, Ashley at first wasn't apologetic at all, increasing his anger to blast-furnace proportion.

"Don't ever walk into my courtroom again!" Daniels shouted at her, pounding his right fist into his left palm for emphasis. "What were you thinking? Wearing that dress in there!"

Ashley had tombstones of fear tumbling across her eyes. She could sense how angry Daniels was.

"I'm so, so sorry," she sobbed. "I had no idea the defense was built on them being fags. I just wore what I wear and didn't even think."

"That's IT," screamed Daniels. "You never think!"

"I think I don't belong in your world," she stammered as she sprinted out the front door.

Daniels' first impulse was to let her go -- realizing that her free spirit was too unbridled for his professional, if not his personal, world. But he was afraid she would get in an accident while driving so angry. So he bolted after her and caught her just as she was opening the door to her car parked in his driveway.

"Let me go!" she screamed, slapping at his arms. "Get the hell away from me!"

Mrs. Palkon, Daniels' 80-year-old neighbor who was as sedate as the Mona Lisa, just happened to be exiting her daughter's car in time to catch Ashley's histrionics. Even though it was dark, Daniels could see, or at least imagine, Mrs. Palkon arching her one eyebrow in disgust.

Daniels quickly overpowered Ashley and soothingly kept repeating: "I'm not letting you drive while you are so upset. Calm down. Then you can go." He kept repeating it as he once recited the rosary as a child. Ashley's screams and flailing finally ebbed into sobs and abject surrender. Daniels escorted her inside the house and she slumped into a living room recliner.

Daniels stood staring at her, conflicted once again by the personal-professional chasm that split his core. Jack Daniels loved Ashley's style and irreverent attitude toward life. John Daniels was appalled by it.

Daniels knew that he had a brewing civil war to stave.

"What am I going to do with you?" he said gently, sitting in the sofa next to her and knowing it would be easier to wrestle with a lobster.

"You will do nothing," she said quietly but defiantly. "You either accept and love me for who I am or you say goodbye. The problem is you are two people. The singer in you loves me. The lawyer in you loathes me. I sure as hell don't want to sound like Sinatra, but I gotta be me. I am not going to change. I don't have to have a filter. You do, at least in your legal world. I'm going home now and you WILL NOT stop me. I will drive calmly and safely. Don't call me for three days. When you do, let me know whether you're in or out. I love Jack but I don't love John. Decide who you are and that decision will dictate whether we're a couple or not."

"It's not that simple," Daniels said.

"Shit, I know it's complicated," she said. "But so are relationships. Think about it and let me know. And if you tell me it's over because John Daniels dominates Jack Daniels, I will understand and never bother you again."

With that, she stood up, leaned over him and kissed his forehead.

"I'm not asking you to give up your practice," she said. "You'd starve as a vocalist, relatively speaking. But I am asking you to be Jack the vocalist who also happens to be a lawyer. Do your job, but not 24/7. Don't let your profession define you. I'm not an idiot. I realize sometimes my behavior in your legal world has been over the top and inappropriate. Down deep, I think I've done that to make a statement, to send a wakeup call to you. Are you damn good as a lawyer? Of course you are. Are you happy as a lawyer? No. Are you happy with me when you're relaxed and rocking on? Of course. I see it in your eyes, hear it in your words, feel it in your body."

With that, she skipped out the door.

Daniels stared at the door for 20 minutes after it closed behind her.

Then he poured himself a Jack Daniels. And then another. An hour later, he kept repeating the same phrase over and over, as if he was chanting. *Who am I? Who am I? Who am I? Who am I?* And all the while playing on an endless loop in his mind was The Who lyric, *Who The Fuck Are You?*

And then he thought about Ashley. What was it about her that attracted him? What was it about that embarrassed him? He knew these were obvious questions with obvious answers. But he was probing deeper into his psyche. He wanted to jam fondue forks into his ears and stir his brain for deeper, psychological answers. Was his obsession with rock and his fascination with Ashley simply symptoms of the long-buried counterculture child residing inside him, screaming to get out? Or was he merely going through a sad midlife crisis? Middle Age Crazy and all that.

And then it hit him with all the force of a wrecking ball to his gut: He *was* two different people, two polar personalities.

One person was the hard-charging professional, a person who wasn't happy unless he was energized and engaged in his work. Whether it be the legal profession or the waste removal racket or putting up circus tents, it was all about work. He thrived on the adrenaline of production. He was a work junkie who defined himself by accomplishment, by achievement. His competitive juices had him soaked in drive. This was John.

The other person was a laid-back, fun-loving, self-indulgent, counterculture rock star with a passion for performing as well as for stimulating, provocative, off-center women. This was Jack. And John had smothered Jack for almost all his life, until recently.

The tension between the two was as sharp as a razor, a dilemma tougher than a $4 sirloin.

And then Daniels had another epiphany, although he hardly was Saul on the road to Damascus. Not that Daniels harbored any pretensions or illusions to divinity, but if God could be three persons in one, why couldn't he be two persons in one? Couldn't he find a balance between John and Jack? Did it have to be such a tightrope act? The chasm didn't have to that gaping if he somehow found a way to blend his wide-ranging personality traits. And there was one characteristic that served as a bridge between John and Jack -- his affinity for performance. He was as much a performer in the courtroom as he was on stage.

Suddenly he knew he could merge his two personalities in one ... but knew that the transition would take time and patience -- two commodities he sometimes ran short on.

Chapter 10

While John and Jack were working on becoming John/Jack or Jack/John depending on the occupation/avocation of the moment, John had to deal with a troubling trend.

John Daniels for years had always gotten the high-end clients in town, like kids of rich folks who got in trouble when they got bored at the country club. But now for the second time in two months, he had lost a potential client to Thaxter Nesbitt. And John heard that in both cases the wealthy daddy of the bad seed felt as if John's credibility had somehow been compromised by his rock singing in local clubs.

This was disturbing on two fronts: Cases involving the rich and locally famous were lucrative. And they were great marketing opportunities. Dirtballs killing dirtballs didn't generate that much publicity unless they wounded at least a dozen innocent suburban bystanders in a High Noon shootout at Fifth and Park streets, the heart of downtown Braxton. But give John a wealthy kid in a high-profile murder, drug or rape case, and it was free advertising.

What also bothered John was that he had no use for Thaxter Nesbitt. Daniels considered Nesbitt to be a sleaze ball who had dropped his ethics when he dropped his first rattle. And John, like many others, thought Nesbitt to be a grandstander in the courtroom. His penchant for over-the-top theatrics and dramatics had cost him more than one big case. So John took great pleasure when both of the wealthy clients who had spurned him were found guilty as the DA's office nailed Nesbitt to the courtroom wall and left him there.

Still, the rock factor impact on Daniels' legal earnings was not to be dismissed lightly. A resolution would have to be found if the John/Jack merger were to be completed successfully.

While John/Jack was busy seeking common ground between his two personalities and between his vocation and avocation, three weeks had fallen from the calendar without him reaching out to Ashley. He had started calling her or texting her countless times but always had stopped short because he really hadn't reached a concrete resolution. He was a mess because he physically ached for her. He knew now that he truly loved her and the biggest regret of his life would be to lose her. But first he had to find himself. He knew he was getting to that destination, but not confident that he had arrived there yet.

As for Ashley, she missed Daniels terribly. And she wasn't totally surprised or deeply hurt that he hadn't contacted her yet. While she didn't know whether he was Jack or John or a combo of both, she did know that he likely would seek a solution before reaching out to her. Ashley wasn't the deep thinker that Daniels was, and that was a blessing for her. Life was easier that way. For instance, Ashley couldn't totally relate to Daniels' personality dilemma. Her rationale was that if ham and cheese could work together in a sandwich, why couldn't John and Jack Daniels work together in a life?

And then it hit her: She needed to save her man from outsmarting himself. It was time for Daniels to dummy down so she no longer had to dummy up. So she immediately texted him with just that:

If ham and cheese can work together in a damn sandwich, why can't John and Jack Daniels work together in a life?

After she sent the text, she laughed and said aloud to herself, "That should make His Esquire think! And realize that I'm not as airy as a soufflé."

Make him think it did. That it did indeed. John was sitting at his office desk, up to his eyeballs in a legal brief. He heard his smartphone chirp and casually checked the message. He had no foreshadowing it would be from Ashley, who hadn't texted him since she walked out of his house.

At first John read the text. Then Jack read it with John. Then they put their heads together. After that they both felt like banging their heads together.

"Man, she's so right!" said John. "We can live and work together. Just compartmentalize."

"Damn!" bellowed Jack. "It ain't all that complicated. Just like three persons in God – if you're a Catholic theologian. We had a gut feeling this was the way to go, but you John always get hung up on all the deeper complications. Lighten up!"

"We can work this out, we can couple John and Jack so Daniels can couple with Ashley again," said John.

"Love that threesome, dude!" exclaimed Jack.

Daniels realized he could no longer risk tearing a labrum while reaching for an excuse for the John/Jack coexistence not to work.

So that was the blueprint. Of course, the devil always is in the details, which traditionally need more divine intervention than mere vision. John and Jack had a vision that Ashley had crystallized in a simple but profound text; now they had to find a way to peacefully coexist so they could see it through.

John/Jack wasted no time in zipping over to Ashley's place, where she greeted the pair with a hug that could have squeezed the waste out of a rhino.

"You are a genius," Daniels said, speaking for both John and Jack. "Life doesn't have to be that complicated. When it's time to be an attorney, I'll be that. That's the ham. When it's time to rock out, I'll be Jack Daniels. That's the cheese. Give and take. And if I have a trial that runs late, rock has to be muted. And if my singing scares away a client or two, screw them!"

"Speaking of screwing, what are you waiting for?" Ashley said moments before they got duly involved in an activity that screws the shit out of either lawyering or singing.

And when they got done making love, they had a drink and made love again. After all, they had to make up for lost time.

Time, by the way, never seems to be on our side. Because it seemingly didn't take much time at all to test the mettle of the newly forged John/Jack professional partnership -- Daniels, Inc., if you will.

Three weeks later John was happier than Jim Morrison on peyote (well, not exactly) when he gave the closing argument in a murder trial that he considered to be a LeBron James slam dunk.

But the jury evidently was dumber than a collection of ash trays as its deliberations stretched to almost 9 p.m. on a Friday night in which Coffeemate was booked to play at 10. Fortunately, someone suddenly must have watered the jurors with Miracle-Gro and their brains sprouted just enough to declare Stanley Slobabinski not guilty of murdering Jose Batista with a meat cleaver even though poor Stanley had been born with two arms that unfortunately ended at his elbows.

In his closing remarks, John had all but said that "Stanley didn't fucking wield that meat cleaver with his fucking toes."

As John raced to the gig at Bunny's Inn in Sorbonne Township, a 15-minute ride from the downtown Braxton courthouse, he realized he hadn't brought a change of clothes for Jack.

So Jack had to sing the first set in a $2500 pin-striped charcoal suit, something Morrison never did. Ashley, ever the trooper, was kind enough to zip to Daniels' house and fetch more appropriate attire for the second set.

Between sets, before he had a chance to change clothes, a local state representative approached Daniels.

58

"Some folks think I'm a tight-assed Republican conservative," said Frank Locker, who was just that. "But I must say that I think it's damn awesome that a respected attorney like you can let your hair down and live out your teen-aged fantasy. Some of my opponents over the years have claimed my childhood fantasy was to be Genghis Khan. But it was to be a rock singer. I sure as hell don't have your voice, John, but would you mind terribly if you and I sang Roy Orbison's *Oh, Pretty Woman* together tonight? It would make my wife so happy."

Locker pointed to his ringside table and Mrs. Locker, who was big enough to be an entire locker room and looked like a woman who was not afraid to step on a cockroach in her bare feet.

"I would be flattered," replied Daniels. "We could be starting a trend. Pretty soon we could have a whole choir of local legislators and lawyers moonlighting in bars at night."

"That wouldn't be a bad idea," said Locker. "All work and no play makes most of us dreary people."

Locker sounded like a guy with a death rattle in his voice during his duet with Daniels, but the crowd ate it up. Even Mrs. Locker stopped eating for a moment to pick up her cell phone and take a picture of her hubby singing with Daniels.

Of course, the picture later went up on Locker's website and it wound up on some other local sites as well.

"At least she didn't post a video on YouTube," Ashley joked to Daniels, who was encouraged that somebody else of some local prominence was fine with going on stage. The John/Jack rollover plan evidently was working. In fact, one tavern owner saw the photo online and booked Coffeemate for a gig.

Ashley was thrilled that the two men in her life, John and Jack, seemed to have entered a state of peaceful co-existence. And she subtly would suggest to John from time to time that

Jack's rocking out relieved stress -- making John even more energetic when was focusing on the law. Granted, she didn't know whether or not this was a valid assumption. But if her spin was working, why not?

Chapter 11

The John/Jack balancing act threatened to fall off the tightrope when Daniels got a call from WBRA Channel 19, the local television station. They wanted to feature the lawyer-by-day, rocker-by-night.

"Well, I'm flattered but I'm not sure I want to do this," Daniels, or rather John, told the producer. "I don't want to give the impression that I don't take my day job seriously."

"We can stress that in the segment," the producer countered. "Besides, a lot of people already know about your double life anyway. And this would be great exposure for your law firm and your band."

"Give me a day to think about it and talk to the guys in the band," Daniels said. "I'll get back to you."

Daniels called Ashley, who, not surprisingly, thought the television segment was a marvelous idea.

"What great exposure for the band," she gushed. "And you can emphasize that your singing doesn't trivialize your lawyering. Some lawyers play golf; others rock on in clubs."

At practice that night Jack told the band. Toad was so excited he almost peed his pants. Bones' Adam's Apple vibrated like his bass strings and his cowlick stood at even more attention than normal. Pudge kept saying that all his piercings and tattoos would look kick ass on TV. Ziggy blinked even more furiously.

"Shit man, it's a no-brainer," Toad said.

"OK," Jack said. "It's a done deal."

"Coffeemate rocks," Pudge bellowed.

WBRA decided to first capture John Daniels the lawyer. Reporter Heather Missonis and a cameraman interviewed Daniels in his law office, where Heather asked a series of routine questions about his academic and legal background, and had him recount some of his more memorable trials.

Then Ms. Missonis threw him a changeup, dropping the softballs and coming in with a hardball right on the hands.

"Do you ever feel guilty about being too good of a lawyer in that your expertise and reputation likely have resulted in many guilty people walking the streets of Braxton?"

But no 25-year-old kid reporter was going to intimidate John Daniels, who had more ice in his veins than he did in his glass of Jack Daniels.

"I have a job to defend people, guilty or not. Everyone has the right to a fair trial. That's all I do."

"Some critics say your trials aren't always fair because you simply overwhelm assistant district attorneys," countered Heather.

"I can't be held accountable for their actions. Our county has many capable assistant district attorneys. Thanks for the flattering assessment of my courtroom skills. But I'm no Perry Mason. Of course, you are way too young to have ever heard of Perry Mason, the famous TV trial lawyer. You probably are too young to remember Jim Morrison."

"The Doors, believe it or not, are my favorite golden-oldies band," she said, blushing.

So, still on camera, John morphed into Jack and sang a few lyrics from *Light My Fire*.

He had done so impulsively but intuitively he realized that he had comfortably and casually cemented the bridge between his lawyer side and his rocker side.

WBRA also got footage of Daniels walking out of the courthouse and of Coffeemate performing at the 3rd & Willow Café.

Heather interviewed Daniels' band mates and didn't get a serious answer from any of them.

"His ego is so enormous he won't even talk to us off stage," Toad claimed.

"He's too important of a man to practice with us, so we just play along listening to Doors' CDs," cracked Pudge.

"Criminals are our biggest fans; they're our groupies. But instead of wanting to sleep with us, they just want Jack, uh, I mean John, to represent them," deadpanned Bones.

"Jack's a lawyer? C'mon, man. I didn't know that," joshed Ziggy.

Heather also talked to some of the customers at the Willow.

"He's sexy as hell, either as a rocker or lawyer," said one middle-aged woman who was wearing too much makeup and too little clothing for her heft.

"Close your eyes and he *is* Jim Morrison," said a guy in his 60s and with the hairline, or lack thereof, to prove it.

"He's the best damn lawyer in town," said a guy who looked like a gangster. "He got my brother off -- twice. And me twice, too. If you're guilty, you gotta call Daniels. I just came out to check out his singing voice. Hard to believe it's the same guy as the lawyer. He's awesome as a singer. Sounds just like Morrison. With talent like that, I don't know why he still works as a lawyer, hanging out with dirtballs."

WBRA obviously got plenty of footage of Jack being Morrison.

Jack did Morrison so passionately that a smitten Heather Missonis whispered hotly to herself, "Just do me."

After getting ample footage, Heather needed a good shower even though she already was wet.

"Awesome, Jack," she gushed like a groupie. "Quit your day job!"

"I would," Jack said with a belly laugh. "But the night job won't pay the rent."

"It will," she proclaimed.

The WBRA segment did help raise his night job pay. Toad and Jack got almost two dozen bookings from clubs throughout eastern Pennsylvania and central New Jersey.

Surprisingly, the TV exposure helped the cash registers ring even louder at his law office. At least a dozen defendants in need of a hotshot attorney who caught the news became clients.

And that's before footage from the segment went on YouTube, where ribbons of vanity video unspool without rhyme or reason.

Suddenly Coffeemate was a firecracker-hot cover band, getting offered gigs from D.C. to Philly to New York to Boston. And folks in need of defendants in the same geographic area were calling for Daniels' legal services.

Meanwhile, every attorney and courthouse employee in Miller County either busted Daniels' balls as if they were walnuts or treated him like, well, a rock star.

Suddenly the *Today Show* and *The Tonight Show Starring Jimmy Fallon* were calling. And not only did they want to interview Daniels, they wanted Coffeemate to perform.

"If I die and go to heaven I won't be any happier than I am now," chirped Toad.

"I'm just glad I'll be sitting behind my drums because guaranteed I'm gonna have a boner on both shows," laughed Pudge.

Bones, meanwhile, was wondering if the two appearances would lead to a guest spot on *America's Got Talent* and Ziggy was wondering if his new-found celebrity would give him a shot at shagging Lindsay Lohan.

"Depends on how screwed up she is at the time," goaded Ashley.

The only band member with some reservations -- can you guess by now, sports fans? -- was Jack (actually John), of course.

"Man, I just hope the judicial system takes me seriously after this," he said.

"Are you freaking kidding me?" snapped Toad. "This will be awesome for the band and for you the celebrity attorney. Hell, if O.J. ever kills somebody again, guaranteed you get the case."

"Hell, you won't need to be a lawyer when we become a great Doors' cover band on the Vegas strip," crowed Bones. "I can't wait. I shoot craps like Winchester shot rifles."

A week later, the Coffeemate band and its unofficial spokesperson, Ashley, were in New York for their *Today* and *The Tonight Show Starring Jimmy Fallon* appearances.

Their *Tonight Show* appearance was first, a taping that started at 5 p.m. on a Tuesday to be aired later that night. While the rest of the band was nervous -- with Bones and Ziggy battling the runs -- Daniels was calm. A lifetime spent in a courtroom dealing with all sorts of dastardly crimes long ago had exterminated all the butterflies in his stomach.

Daniels was the second guest of the evening and he alone sat down to be interviewed by Jimmy Fallon. The band was off to the side of the studio, awaiting Daniels to join them and perform *Light My Fire* after his chat with the host.

"So do you think Jim Morrison is rolling over in his grave over the fact that an impersonator is a lawyer by day?" cracked Fallon.

"Nah, he probably wished I was around to help him beat that indecent exposure charge rap in Miami," replied Daniels.

That line genuinely caught Fallon as hilarious.

"So have you ever exposed yourself on stage?" countered Fallon.

"Man, the DA's office would throw me in Miller County Prison and throw away the key," laughed Daniels. "I've spent too much time, uh, beating the pants off them."

Fallon now was laughing so hard he may have peed his pants under his desk.

When he had regained his composure, Fallon said: "You must be quite the criminal defense attorney."

"I'm thinking about having the words *Not Guilty* tattooed on my forehead," Daniels grinned.

"Hope you're not this funny in the courtroom," Fallon said.

With his band members and Ashley amazed and impressed with how casual, smooth and funny he was, Daniels suddenly got serous to emphasize how his legal integrity was in no way compromised by his dalliance with rock and roll.

"Definitely not," Daniels said. "The right to a fair trial is something I cherish deeply and it's my sincere honor to be part of such an esteemed judicial process."

"All righty, counselor," Fallon summed up the chat. "Now let's hear you sing Jim Morrison. Ladies and gentlemen, I give you Coffeemate!"

Morrison and Coffeemate -- even with Bones and Ziggy squeezing their ass cheeks together -- nailed *Light My Fire* better than they ever had.

After the song, Fallon bounded up to the band and proclaimed: "This is Jim Morrison and The Doors come back to life!"

It was a television appearance that showcased what an amazing palette of gifts Daniels was blessed with, and it further fertilized the pollination of his two distinct personalities.

Ashley was so excited she almost made love to Daniels right there in the studio, in front of Jimmy Fallon and a whole country full of viewers.

Toad had tears in his eyes when he hugged Daniels and said solemnly, "You're the best thing that has ever happened to me. We can make this gig go big time and you still can find time for your legal shit."

Jack was certain Toad was right while John also was starting to believe it more than ever.

"Damn right," Pudge said. "Pick and choose whatever rocks your boat. And if rocking and lawyering rock your boat, well, get your rocks off!"

"Let's go party," Ziggy shouted.

"Nope. We got get our rest for the *Today Show* tomorrow," Toad said. "That's a damn early wakeup and we don't want to look hung over."

"Absolutely," Daniels said. "We just won the first game of a doubleheader. Tomorrow we close the show. Wonder if we'll have Matt Lauer interviewing us?"

When they got back to their Manhattan hotel room. Ashley hugged Daniels so tightly his ribs almost cracked.

"You, sir, were sensational tonight," she said, delightedly. "You are so much the lawyer and the rocker. You do both so well!"

"And finally I'm comfortable doing both, Ash," Daniels said. "I've come to realize both are very important to me. Both parts of me. It's who I am. And I've come to realize that you are most important of all. And you are the one who bridged John and Jack."

"Do me, babe!" Ashley yelped.

Suffice it to say, Daniels did precisely that.

The next day dawned dark and ominous with thunderstorms forecast. The *Today Show* nevertheless opted to have Coffeemate perform outside as part of its concert in the street series. The band was covered by a canopy in case of a storm, but the large audience was not. Coffeemate was to perform a song; then Daniels was to be interviewed by Savannah Guthrie.

During a commercial break just prior to Coffeemate's song, Guthrie remarked to Daniels that the size of the crowd exceeded their expectations because Coffeemate was not a big-name band like they usually booked.

"It had to be your Jimmy Fallon appearance last night," Guthrie said. "You and the band were sensational. We got a big walkup crowd this morning. Just hope the weather holds off."

"Looks pretty bleak," Daniels said.

He called over Toad.

"Toad and Savannah, let's start with *Light My Fire* but segue quickly into *Riders On The Storm*," he said.

They both thought that was perfect.

Two minutes into *Light My Fire* the heavens opened up and while some of the crowd sprinted for cover, some of it remained standing and got soaked, riveted by Daniels and Coffeemate. And when the band abruptly switched to *Riders On The Storm*, the thunder wasn't the only thing roaring. The crowd went crazy -- wet and wild crazy!

When Coffeemate finished playing, Guthrie, obviously thrilled with the performance and the crowd reaction, was as effusive as a 13-year-old.

"That simply was amazing," she gushed on air. "Jack, you sound like Jim Morrison. Almost as if Morrison, or at least his voice, has come back from the dead. And your band sounds just like The Doors."

"Thanks," replied Daniels, grinning dimples.

"I also understand you are quite the criminal defense attorney back home in Braxton, PA. How on earth do you manage to do both?" Guthrie asked, continuing the on-air interview.

"Well, it can be a challenge at times when my night job and day job scrape fenders," Daniels said. "But I've gotten better at navigating both pursuits, driving in both lanes without getting hung up on the median barrier. Both the law and music are great passions of mine. And in a sense, you are as much a performer in the courtroom as you are on stage."

"If I ever get a speeding ticket driving through Braxton, I want you to get me off," Guthrie said without realizing the alternate connotation.

Of course, Daniels, Coffeemate and the rest of America picked up on it instantly.

"It would be my pleasure," quickly responded Daniels.

Suddenly Guthrie's face became redder than the Red Sea, which, by the way, really isn't red.

"I plead guilty," proclaimed the now-giddy Guthrie. "But first this is *Today* on NBC."

The merger of John and Jack Daniels had been fully consummated by the back-to-back appearances on network television.

The exposure was more priceless than quarter-inch hex nuts.

Their future as a band glittered like a jewel box awash in moonlight.

But now the real challenges loomed as large as the setting sun on the Pacific horizon. Coffeemate had been plunged deep into the media fishbowl and the tides the immersion triggered could prove to be a real tsunami headed right for the tightrope Daniels straddled. More than ever he would need his lifeline, the comely and seductive Ashley Dupree.

Chapter 12

Daniels and Coffeemate were immediately besieged with offers.

Jack Steele, a promoter specializing in retro rock acts, called Daniels and offered to put the band on a national tour --10 tour stops at $30,000 for each concert.

"I almost swallowed my Adam's Apple when I heard those dollars," Bones said.

"How can you swallow something that's already in your throat?" Pudge asked.

"That's why I didn't," Bones replied, as if the logic was transparent.

No Longer Virgin Records, a small record label specializing in producing CDs for cover bands with strong regional followings, wanted Coffeemate in the studio immediately, if not sooner.

People magazine broke its rule of covering only celeb teen-agers and called Daniels for an interview and photo shoot.

"Do it," Ashley commanded him. "They get *People* magazine at the beauty salon."

Toad, Bones, Pudge and Ziggy all wanted to ditch their day jobs and take Coffeemate as far as they could. They all were smitten with a there-will-definitely-be-a-pony-under-the-tree optimism.

Of course, their day jobs weren't exactly professional, or lucrative, in nature. They weren't exactly floating in a river of corporate ooze. Regarding employment, they all worked as well as a Styrofoam hammer.

Toad now worked as a clerk in a gun gallery, joking with Jack that some of Daniels' best clients practiced their craft there.

Bones worked in a factory where he soldered wires.

Pudge worked in a meat manufacturing plant, slaughtering pigs.

Ziggy worked in a music store, sorting guitar strings.

Meanwhile, Daniels again was torn apart by this golden opportunity. He didn't have or want a partner in his law firm. So if he went full tilt after rock stardom, he would have to severely curtail his practice or hang up his shingle. And as much as the prospect of Coffeemate going full-time excited Jack, it gave John gas pains.

So once again he felt trapped on that tightrope, losing his balance over a Sophie's choice. For years he had identified himself as a litigator. It was intrinsic to him. The law was embedded in his DNA. And then there was the once-in-a-life opportunity to be the rock star he always had wanted to be and part of him wanted to squeeze it until the juice ran down his arms and legs, with apologies to Led Zeppelin.

"What the hell am I going to do?" he lamented one night in bed.

"You are wrestling so hard with this that you haven't wrestled with me in four nights," Ashley said, exasperated. "Do you realize that? You know, you make bigger problems out of this than there really are."

"It's only the entire direction of my future, our future," Daniels said, frustrated.

He sat up in bed. Ashley could see tears in his eyes and the effect was as contagious as swine flu. She teared up in a hiccup, and kissed him sweetly on his forehead.

"OK, hotshot, listen to what I think," she purred. "You have had a dream to be a rock star your whole life. A dream, until recently, that you snuffed out because you also have a calling to the law that runs thicker than some of your damn law books. You are a gifted singer and a gifted litigator. You still can rock and lawyer up, just on a bigger stage. You still can be John and Jack, and they both can be bigger than ever. Pursue the big time with Coffeemate. Your band members deserve that. They don't have the privileges of your life. This means everything to them. So why not do this full-time and still practice law?"

"That's impossible," he interrupted. "I can't be on tour and in Miller County Courthouse at the same time."

"You can't," she said. "So don't be silly. Close your Braxton practice. Open one in L.A. and become a criminal defense attorney for celebrities. Just handle marquee cases when they arise and concentrate on your music most of the time. Defending celebs with oodles of money will be lucrative and generate residual business because their cases are so high profile. But pick your cases so you can tour and record. With your impeccable legal credentials, your new-found fame, your poise and personality ... well, you can take your legal career to a whole new level while leaving behind the steady stream of dirtballs that wash up against your Braxton office door."

She looked at Daniels, wondering how many heads he saw while looking back at her.

"Think I'm such sort of two-headed monster for saying that?" she asked.

Daniels remained silent for only a few minutes, even though to her if felt like an eternity and a day.

"You know, not all celebrity cases are bullshit," he said, rolling the concept around in his brain to see if it picked up any lint. "Not that some of my cases here aren't bullshit. And God knows, I'm sick of the basic criminal element, especially those who have trouble paying their attorney. At least celebrities usually have some cash flow. And one career could help the other, that's for sure. But suppose Coffeemate goes on tour and cuts a record ... and then flames out? As good as we are as a cover band, that's all we are. And original artists become stars, not cover artists. Plus, a lot of the media interest in us is simply because I'm an attorney. If I essentially put my litigation career on the back burner, what makes us stand out?"

"OK, talk yourself out of your dream," Ashley scolded. "And regret it forever. Listen, you already climbed the mountaintop as a lawyer in Braxton. What else is there to do here? Now you can take your legal career into another exciting dimension. But most of all, pursue the music. And who says you have to be just a cover band? Lawyers write. You are a creative guy. You and the band can do some originals."

"Brains and beauty," Daniels said, smiling broadly. "You are the total package."

"Just don't suck when you go on tour," Ashley laughed. "Unless, of course, you're sucking face with me!"

"We'll leave the groupies to my band mates," Daniels joked.

"I'd pay to see that," Ashley giggled.

"You couldn't pay me to see that!" he spat out between chuckles.

The next night Daniels told his Coffeemate sidekicks that while he was all for pursuing a tour and an opportunity with the record label, the practical situation was he first had to clear his legal calendar, one that included two trials, one of them a murder trial, in the next month.

Needless to say, that went over with the boys like a piranha in a vodka bottle. They, of course, would have it much easier to cut ties with their day jobs. In fact, they wouldn't even need scissors.

"You're being selfish!" snapped Toad, who just couldn't see how hard it would be for Daniels to watch the dusk fade on his legal practice.

"Get another lawyer to fill in," commanded Pudge. "There must a thousand of them in town."

"Have your clients all plead guilty since they are anyway," cracked Bones. "They all are just a useless wad of pre-chewed pork gristle."

"If you got run over by a truck, your clients would have to find another lawyer," said Ziggy. "Tell them you just got run over by a train of opportunity."

Daniels looked them all in the eye and realized he couldn't deny their dream of the Big Time. Damn it, neither could he.

"Listen guys," he said. "I do want to do this. Let's finalize the deal with the record label and start recording a CD in a month. We can seal the deal for the tour, which won't start right away for obvious reasons. So it should all work out. We just have to find the time to practice as much as possible and perhaps think about some original material. We can't do all covers. Toad, you think of what Morrison and The Doors would be doing today and let's try to capture that."

"You ain't just stringing us along, are you?" asked Pudge, arching an eyebrow.

"Hell, no," Daniels exclaimed. "Who wouldn't want to be Jim Morrison come back to life?"

Chapter 13

The next couple weeks were a whirlwind for Daniels. He and Coffeemate practiced more intensely than ever and did six local gigs, packed to the rafters as their new-found celebrity trailed them like a timber wolf.

Meanwhile, Daniels won his first of two trials that month, an armed robbery case that even a public defender who had to take the bar exam a dozen times likely wouldn't have screwed up. His second trial was a murder case in which his 19-year-client was accused of, while 8 months pregnant, of murdering her estranged boyfriend by shooting him between the eyes with his own Glock as he beat her with a frying pan. He figured that if he couldn't get her off on self defense, he definitely should hang up his legal shingle and pretend to be Morrison for the remainder of his life.

In the midst of all this work, Daniels tried to find at least an hour of quality time with Ashley each day, or rather, night. He had grown to love her more and more and was totally grateful for her counsel and insight on how best to bridge the chasm between his legal and music passions. Of course, that tightrope act intruded on their time together but Ashley was so into the final fusion of John and Jack, she didn't mind.

Most of Daniels' legal colleagues were supportive of his decision to dismantle his Miller County practice because many of them had seen his appearance on *The Tonight Show* and *Today* and realized how much singing talent he actually had.

But a few of them thought that he was being frivolous.

One of them was Judge Nathan Hawthorne.

"You know I love The Doors and having heard you sing on national television, I swear you are Jim Morrison," Hawthorne said to Daniels outside the Miller County Courthouse one afternoon. "But still, you have such a wonderful gift as a litigator. You are an extraordinary criminal defense attorney and you serve a vital community function. Everybody, even the guilty, deserves an excellent lawyer. Your defection to Hollywood is going to leave a void here. Besides, not all criminal defense attorneys are as ethical as you."

"Thank you, Judge," said Daniels, truly touched. "But this is a dream that will turn into a nightmare if I don't at least pursue it. And if for some other reason the dream turns into a nightmare, there is no law saying that I can't come back here and practice."

"Unless you expose yourself on stage and get disbarred," joked the judge.

Daniels also was touched when he got a phone call from the mother of a former client of his. The young man had been charged with rape at a fraternity party at a local college, Kulptown University, but had been the victim of mistaken identity. The coed, who was drunk at the time of the sexual assault, confused Daniels' client with another KU student who bore a strong resemblance. The latter had Type-O blood compared to the defendant's AB. The police report failed to note that the rape victim had specks of Type-O blood under her fingernails from scratching her assailant's genitals. Her frantic clawing had left a small, jagged scar on one of his testicles. When Daniels displayed an enlarged photo of that student's scarred left nut (which the kid had given to another KU coed, an image she shared with the defense team) while Daniels had the actual rapist on the witness stand, the boy cracked like an egg and confessed.

"My son would have been in jail for years if you hadn't been so smart and diligent," said the mother of the boy who had been falsely charged. "Did you know he now is in his third-year of law school and wants to be a criminal defense attorney just like you? You saved his life and you are his role model. Do you want to give that up to be a singer? If people want to listen to Jim Morrison, they can just download a Doors' CD."

The phone call did give Daniels pause but he knew that ultimately this was about him. After all, there were others out there who served as lifelines.

Ashley, meanwhile, was searching online for a place for her and Daniels to rent when they moved to L.A. They were practically living together now and they would make it full-time, especially with Ashley out of work with the move. The question was where the Coffeemate band mates were going to live. They didn't have enough money to live separately because they couldn't yet count on money from the tour or record deal, details that had to be finalized. Toad had suggested they temporarily all live with Ashley and Daniels, plus some of them actually had girlfriends who could be seen in public. Ashley thought it was a great idea but Daniels almost choked on his tuna sandwich when she ran Toad's idea past him.

"That would be a freaking commune," Daniels yelped. "None of their girlfriends!"

"It would be only temporary until Coffeemate hits it big and the guys can afford their own digs," Ashley countered.

"That's a big if," Daniels said.

"Another complication about our move to L.A. is if I am going to practice law regularly in California, I must be a member of the bar," Daniels said. "It's been a long time since I took the bar exams in Pennsylvania and New Jersey. If we are in the recording studio and on the road, it's going to be tough to brush up for the bar exam. And God forbid John Daniels flunks it. It will get a lot of ink, like JFK Jr. kept flunking the New York bar."

"You worry too much," Ashley soothed. "Everything will work out. Besides, you're no JFK Jr. He had better hair."

"Hair or not, sometimes I look in the mirror and wonder if I'm John Daniels, Jack Daniels or the ghost of Jim Morrison."

"Stop thinking and start making love to me," Ashley said while unbuttoning her blouse. "You have too little time for hanky-panky these days."

"I always make time for that! I may be crazy but I'm not insane."

The next night Coffeemate held a practice session and all agreed they had never sounded better. Daniels could sense that everybody was taking their game to the next level in anticipation of the tour and the recording session. Toad, Bones and Ziggy all had written original material that all of them thought captured the sounds of The Doors and could be tracks on the CD and fresh additions to their playlist. All of which left Daniels feeling that somehow he could not allow his legal workload to intrude on all of their big-time dreams.

He also more and more was realizing that his strong sense of self would steel his transition to big-time rock star. After all, egotism is not something you develop over dinner ... like a tattoo, it's etched into the flesh.

"No pressure here," Daniels texted Ashley during a break.

Daniels had about three hours sleep a night for the next couple weeks because he had to be busier than a one-armed paperhanger with the crabs to finish up his legal loose ends in Braxton. Pending cases had to find new homes as he and his secretary transferred clients to several law firms -- all of them eager to gobble them up.

"Your competitors had been starving to death because all the attractive and not-so attractive clients always came to you," said his secretary, Helen Thomas, a 60-year-old dynamo who now was going to retire and spend time with her nine grandchildren. "Only the clients who couldn't rub two nickels together didn't call us."

"Unfortunately some of these clients are going to find out that not all defense attorneys were created equal," Daniels said with a chuckle. "You, your grandchildren and all the criminal defense attorneys in town all are thrilled that I'm hanging up my shingle in Braxton."

"Once you and Ashley find a home in L.A., my husband and I are coming to visit you for a week," Helen said.

"You are more than welcome because I will put you to work as I eventually set up shop there," Daniels replied. "First you can study for the California bar for me so I can concentrate on my music."

"There goes your law career, so you had better be the next Jim Morrison," she laughed.

However, on the road to becoming the next Morrison, a big detour developed the day before the Coffeemate gang was to depart for L.A. for the CD recording sessions.

The 19-year-old son of the mayor of Braxton was charged with the rape and murder of the 17-year-old daughter of the police chief of Braxton. Compounding matters, the mayor and the chief had been feuding for several years. The mayor immediately told the media that he suspected that police planted evidence to railroad his son. The police chief and the district attorney emphatically denied the mayor's allegations.

Bottom line, even a blind man could read that this sensational case, perhaps the biggest and juiciest in the history of Braxton, had John Daniels' name scrawled all over it.

Even as the story immediately went viral online and became a hot read nationwide, the mayor was on the phone asking Daniels to represent his son, who was an idiot at first and declined legal representation until the courts assigned him a temp public defender who got his law degree from a school that recruits on the back of a pack of matches. Of course, his old man also gently persuaded him to change his mind when he casually mentioned he would have him neutered and butchered and cut out of the will.

"What the hell do you mean you're moving to L.A.?" screamed Mayor Albert Swanson, fear suddenly spreading in his gut like wet cement. "I need you here! My son Biff needs you here. The dumb bastard at first didn't even want a lawyer. He then got stuck with some public defender who hasn't started shaving yet and who wore sneakers to the arraignment. And he looks like a real pussy."

"Albert, you don't understand," Daniels said, who suddenly wasn't so sure he wanted to leave town, being the sudden victim of an emotional jackknifing. "I have to record an album out there with my rock band and then go on tour."

"Man, you can't be freaking serious about that crap," Swanson bellowed. "You're the best damn criminal lawyer in town."

"Hire one from out of town," Daniels said. "I can give you some names."

"They don't know the politics of this town," Swanson said. "This murder/rape rap is politically motivated. Fat Fucking Driscoll is a crooked police chief and he's doing this to me, to Biff, because I was about to blow the whistle on him."

"Fred Driscoll actually has a sterling reputation," Daniels countered.

"Bullshit! I've uncovered something on Saint Fred that will curl your eyebrows and split your nut sack!" Swanson barked.

"Split my nut sack? What will all those groupies on tour think of me?"

"Don't get cute with me, Daniels," Swanson screamed. "My son is in a pile of shit that he didn't jump into. He was shoved into it. And you are the only guy who can shovel him out. Plus, to be frank, this would be the biggest damn case of your career. Win this one and your legend as a litigator will be etched into the courthouse building. And then you can go pretend you're a rock star."

A jolt of electricity shot down Daniels' spine, followed by a jolt of dread. This was the trial of a lifetime and a large part of him couldn't walk away from this. But an equally large part of him couldn't walk away from his Coffeemate commitments, to squander recording and tour opportunities that likely wouldn't be there in several months. And he couldn't force his band mates to walk away from their dreams.

"It would take months for the trial to happen and I can't put my musical commitments on hold for that long," Daniels said. "It's simply not practical. Under normal circumstances, I would jump at the chance to defend your son."

"Yeah, before your midlife crisis hit. Fuck you!"

With that, Swanson ended the call. But not Daniels' dilemma. John/Jack, actually just John, looked into a mirror and asked himself: "What the fuck?"

When Daniels told Ashley about the call from the mayor, she freaked.

"You're not gonna cave on this, are you?" she asked loud enough to be confused with a sonic boom. "That ship has sailed. I know what a plum trial that would be for you, although I hate myself for using that term in what was such a horrible crime. That poor young girl. How atrocious!"

"As I said, I told the mayor no. An emphatic no. It's just not practical. Damn, under different circumstances, I would jump on this. But not now. I can't back out on our musical dreams. It would devastate the Coffeemate guys. And me. And you. And there's no freaking way I could do both and do justice to both careers."

"You actually thought about trying to pull off that impossible balancing act?" Ashley asked, her eyes bigger than manhole covers.

"Well, sort of," admitted Daniels. "The trial wouldn't start for months. After our recording session, I still could research the trial while we are on tour. It would be crazy though."

"Hell yeah, it would," she screamed. "You would have to be insane to try that. And the mayor and his son would have to be insane to let a part-time lawyer handle their case."

"So it won't happen," Daniels said. "I'm at peace with this."

"Your face looks anything but peaceful," Ashley said. "Put this behind you the moment we take off for L.A. tomorrow. And don't mention this to Toad and the guys."

"They would jam all their instruments up my ass for sure," Daniels joked. But his face wasn't smiling.

And that face of his was frowning moments later when his phone rang again. It was Barney Higgins, the chief county commissioner of Miller.

Everything was becoming such a chaotic cacophony of confusion.

"John, this horrible murder-rape case is one of the low moments in our county's history," Higgins said. "It is so tragic for the Driscoll and Swanson families. And a terrible blight on our entire community. I have no idea of knowing whether the Swanson kid is guilty or was set up, as alleged by our mayor. While Al Swanson and I have been friends and Democratic political cronies for years, that is irrelevant. I just think for the sake of our community that the Swanson boy is entitled to the best legal representation available. You!"

"Thank you for the kind words, Barney. But I'm leaving town. Tomorrow. As I told Al Swanson, there are excellent criminal defense attorneys elsewhere. He can get a top-notch guy from Philly. With the trial months away, the attorney can get up to speed on the dynamics of Braxton. This is such a high-profile case, and with the allegations by the mayor against the police chief, perhaps an out-of-town jury or a change of venue would be appropriate. Which would mean nobody on the jury would know or care whether John Daniels or John Hancock was the defense attorney."

"Right now the DA is saying he doesn't want an out-of-town jury or a change of venue," Higgins said.

"What can I say? I am committed to these musical obligations," Daniels said.

Higgins sighed and added: "I'd say grow up but you already have grown up into a mid-life crisis."

"I keep hearing that. But this is not a lark at all. It's a new beginning. We all have to do what's best for us."

"OK, be happy," Higgins said. "I hope you are doing what's best for you."

"So do I."

Ashley was listening to the conversation and when Daniels hung up, she simply said: "You have to live your life for you, not for others. There's a bigger world out there than this town. I never read anywhere that Braxton is the epicenter of the universe."

"It's done, we're leaving tomorrow and that's it," Daniels said, giving her a gentle hug and kiss.

The next day dawned dark, dreary and wet. Daniels had hired a limo service to transport the band, Ashley, himself and their luggage and musical instruments/gear to the Philadelphia Airport in a bus. Although it was raining so hard it looked as if they were driving through a car wash, the mood inside the bus was bright, sunny and cheerful. The Coffeemate guys, including Daniels, were all pumped up, as was Ashley.

Then Toad had to open his mouth.

"Man, that murder-rape of the police chief's daughter was something," he said to Daniels. "And they charged the mayor's son. It was all over the *Braxton Bugle* front page this morning. Betcha you'd love to defend him."

Daniels quietly responded with: "Under different circumstances, hell yes. But not now. We are a band and we are going to rock on to the top."

"The mayor called him to represent his son and Jack turned him down," Ashley said.

Toad, suddenly looking as pensive and stern as a trial judge, asked, "But is John Daniels OK with that?"

Daniels smiled and quickly said, "Both Jack and John are fine with it. Hell, if I could have it both ways and do the recording sessions and do the tour and prepare for the trial; that would be great. But that's impossible. My courtroom days in Braxton are over. I'm working full-time with you guys and later on in my spare time I may do some celebrity cases in Hollywood. So once you guys become stars and get busted, I'll be there for you. At a righteous price."

"Fuck you," laughed Toad, looking relieved. As did the rest of the band. And Ashley. And Jack. But perhaps not John.

Chapter 14

Braxton Mayor Albert Swanson pitched his son Biff's defense to almost a dozen prominent criminal defense attorneys in Philadelphia and Manhattan and struck out more often than Reggie Jackson did. Some of the attorneys were booked solid; others were simply too pricey for a mayor with Swanson's less than six-figure salary.

Compounding matters, his son was giving Swanson all kinds of grief. The mayor thought his son was innocent and his son swore that he was. Still, the kid told his old man that he was shitting his pants worrying that political opponents of his father on the jury might be only too willing to make his kid fry.

"Biff, more than half the people in this town are Latino and don't even know who the hell I am," Swanson lied. "Nobody votes in this town. The Latinos hold no grudges against me."

Desperate and scared shitless that matters were going to hell with a seat next to the furnace, the mayor decided it was time for a bold move.

He decided to fire Fred Driscoll as police chief, which was his right as mayor. He was going to cite police misconduct, claiming that Driscoll was receiving kickbacks from several top city drug dealers for looking the other way. The mayor thought he had some evidence that might link Driscoll to being a dirty cop, but what evidence he had at that point still was circumstantial and incomplete. He was gambling that where there was smoke there was fire. Besides, the firing would spark one blazing firestorm by itself.

Swanson decided to run the idea by Big Jim Gallagher, the veteran DA who was a no-nonsense prosecutor that the crime-ridden community routinely reelected.

Gallagher found the idea as shocking as watching a cute cat leap from his lap to dismember a bird.

"Are you freaking insane?" Gallagher screamed at Swanson, poking him in the chest. "You do that and you have convicted your son. Pull this dumb shit and compared to Biff, Custer was even money. Even if this trial would be taken out of town, a jury there still will be prejudiced by your firing of the police chief. You should not do this for the sake of your son."

"How do you know that? If I can prove that Driscoll is a dirty cop, people will realize that he is framing my son," Swanson yelled back.

"That is one freaking big stretch," Gallagher said. "Trust me, you would be handing me this case on a silver platter. Already it's probable that Biff gets convicted. You would turn that into a slam dunk if you do this. Hell, I shouldn't even be talking to you about this case."

Swanson, even though he looked as though he had just caught a spear in the groin, would not relent.

"Get your damn office on the stick and see what you can find out about Driscoll and some kickbacks from drug dealers," commanded the mayor.

"Relax, Albert," Gallagher said, lowering his tone. "I will but you are not my boss. I'm frankly dubious about your allegations because all the top drug dealers I know of around here hate cops and would never, ever deal with them. They don't trust cops. And they would never give their money to a cop. These Latino gang leaders are not like the Italian Mafia. You need to get out in the street more."

"Find me something, anything," Swanson said.

"Again, I shouldn't even be talking to you since my office will wind up prosecuting your son if the trial is held in Braxton," Gallagher said. "This is a conflict of interest."

"Fuck that," Swanson said. "This is my son we are talking about. Screw ethics."

The next day the mayor decided to screw Fred Driscoll and fire him as police chief. At a hastily arranged press conference, he pulled no punches in calling Driscoll a dirty cop but pulled his punches when it came to specifics.

When pressed for details by an aggressive *Braxton Bugle* reporter, Albert Swanson said the investigation was ongoing and a detailed list of violations would be available once Driscoll was charged.

When Gallagher found out that the impulsive Swanson had terminated Driscoll, he uttered a belly laugh and sarcastically remarked to his secretary: "What a dumb bastard! His sorry ass will be fried when no charges against his former police chief are forthcoming."

Of course, the media flocked to Gallagher and Driscoll for comment. Both men were blunter than a Billy club to the gut with their responses.

Driscoll's only response was a terse "I'm only guilty of one thing -- working for an asshole who's dumber than a fire plug. Piss on him!"

Gallagher cracked that "My office obviously will investigate the mayor's allegation, but I suspect the only thing we'll find is that the mayor, already a crazy man, now has totally gone insane."

When pressed if he could prosecute Swanson's son without bias after saying the mayor was crazy, the DA smiled and calmly said: "Of course, I have integrity. Evidently the mayor wasn't standing in the same line when they handed out integrity. As for Chief Driscoll, he is an impeccable cop and if I were his legal counsel, I would advise him to sue the pants off Al Swanson and then wait for the voters to throw the mayor out on his naked ass."

The following day, Daniels, Ashley and the band were unpacking boxes in their rented Santa Monica condo when county commissioner Barney Higgins called Daniels' cell and told him the mayor had fired the police chief and detailed the firestorm it had ignited.

"If there was ever a time a kid needed justice and a great lawyer, it's now," Higgins told Daniels. "Once Swanson tossed Driscoll on the street, he also tossed his son on death row."

Higgins figured that his call would get Daniels' attention like a crowbar to the nuts. He figured wrong. He thought he was talking to John Daniels. But this was L.A., not Braxton. And it fast was becoming more the new hometown of Jack Daniels, not John Daniels.

"A year ago, Barney, I would have gotten such a hard-on over such a delicious case that I could have pogo-sticked on my cock cross country," Daniels said, laughing. "But I have a new life now, a new opportunity. If there was ever a time a guy needed to follow his lifelong dream, it's now. Braxton now is in my rear view mirror. So I'm not the guy to save the ass of the mayor's kid."

Higgins' exhale of exasperation sounded like the whoosh of a balloon emptying.

"You're seeing stars there in Hollywood and it's blinding you," Higgins said. "You still can pretend to be Jim Morrison on stage and in the recording studio when you need to be while working the case here. You already have Morrison, pardon the pun, down cold. How much fucking prep time do you need? Hell, even when you were handling major murder trials here, you still worked on numerous other cases. You were up to your ass in guilty bastards and you had no choice not to work your ass off. Besides, this case will get national attention and all the publicity will boost your singing career. The only reason people give a fuck about your Morrison knockoff act is because you're a lawyer. Otherwise you're just another lounge singer doing covers."

Daniels was silent for a few minutes that seemed frozen in time. Higgins knew he had struck a nerve, just like his dentist often did to him.

"Let me think about it and run some crazy logistics through my head," Daniels said. "Of course, this could all be a moot point. Because if I decide to do the trial, my girlfriend and the guys in the band are going to impale my nuts on the Hollywood sign."

After Daniels hung up, he was hung up on what Higgins said. There was no question that Coffeemate hitched a ride on the strong winds of opportunity because it was hitched to the wagon of Daniel's day job. Uniqueness sells. And with the publicity generated from a trial like Biff Swanson's would mean great exposure in the social media and conventional media. But Daniels did need to rehearse with the band for the album and the tour. It wasn't as if he were singing alone in the shower.

Daniels exhaled again, knowing that if he did opt to do the case, it would be a tougher sell to Ashley and the band than selling central air conditioning to Eskimos. And he also knew he had to make a decision in a day or two to get on top of the case. And there always was the possibility that the mayor would secure a good attorney in the interim. For now, a public defender was handling the case. But that was like letting a piano tuner defuse a bomb. It was sort of clumsy and things could blow up in your face.

There was no time for further reflection because Ashley and Pudge entered the room, wondering why Daniels was goldbricking.

"Just because you're the lead singer, you still unpack boxes," Ashley said, laughing. "No divas around here. Except for me."

She rushed up to Daniels and kissed him on the lips, squealing: "I've never been happier!"

Daniels needed the sheer force of will to make himself smile. And when he did, it was a half-assed smile. Sort of like when the moon was just a sliver.

Ashley quickly picked up on Daniels' sudden mood shift. He had been rather euphoric before his cell rang and he walked in an adjoining room.

"Well, I don't have to be fucking Sherlock Holmes to deduce that the call was about that damn murder trial, right?" she snapped, her eyeballs spitting embers like a camp fire.

"Yes. It was Barney Higgins. He said the community needs me to take this trial, just not for the sake of the mayor and his kid. He said I could still prep the band for the tour and the CD and find the time to prepare a case and arrange my schedule here around a trial date. He said the prime reason for Coffeemate's appeal as a Doors cover band was me being a lawyer. And if I no longer am a lawyer, we're just another lounge act."

"That's simply not true," Ashley said. "He's just trying to sell you on something that's impossible to do. You can't do that kid justice and do the band, not to mention yourself, justice if you do both."

"I know that," Daniels said, "and I'm not going to do it. So relax. Braxton is behind me. But I wonder if there isn't some element of truth into what Higgins was saying."

"What the hell does some county commissioner who's a pig farmer know about what makes a star a star?" Ashley said. "Of course there are cover bands everywhere. But you are special. You sound so much like Morrison that you ARE Morrison when you are on stage. And the band is incredibly talented. I know they don't look it, but they *sound* it! And I can't wait to hear some of the original tracks you guys will develop. If you can do originals as well as covers, you are much more than just a cover band. You are not just some Morrison impersonator appearing at the Braxton Fair!"

"Damn, you should be a motivational speaker," Daniels said, this time flashing a smile strong enough to hang wash on. "You're right! And don't mention this to the guys."

"Of course not. They'd cut your dick off. And I've become attached to it."

"Not as much as I have," Daniels laughed.

The next day Ashley, Daniels and the Coffeemate guys met with Cy Schwartzman, their agent and conduit to their record label, No Longer Virgin Records, and their tour promoter Moe Katz Productions.

Schwartzman's Burbank office was a tad garish, with replica gold records hanging so low from the ceiling that only midgets could walk without ducking. Of course, Cy at 5-foot-1 could pass for a tall midget.

"Welcome to L.A., boys and girl," boomed Schwartzman, who always spoke in decibel levels rivaling that of a heavy metal band. "You guys are gonna be stars and we're all gonna be rich. Of course, I'm already rich."

"Money can't buy me love," said Pudge Klumpf, Coffeemate's massive drummer.

"Trust me," bellowed Schwartzman, "when you're out on tour you'll get all the love you need."

Schwartzman laughed and then pointed to Ziggy Zmroczek, their rhythm guitarist/pipsqueak, and cracked: "Well, maybe not him!"

Ziggy turned even paler and smiled meekly.

"Just joshing you, pal," Schwartzman said in a very unapologetic tone.

"Speaking of the tour, did you get any dates firmed up yet?" asked Daniels.

"Well," hedged Schwartzman, "there's been a slight delay. Tootsie Jones, who is booking dates for Moe Katz Productions, has had a little trouble lining up enough venues. She's looking at small to medium places and only has three booked so far. She wants at least a half-dozen lined up before the tour commences."

"What towns are booked?" asked Ashley, looking concerned.

"The Performing Arts Center in your hometown of Braxton, PA; an arena in Trenton, New Jersey; and a performing arts center in Wilmington," Schwartzman responded.

"What the hell did we come all the way to L.A. for if we're only performing close to home?" asked Toad, the band leader and lead guitarist.

"Relax," Cy said. "Other booking dates are forthcoming. Delicate negotiations are ongoing. By the way, Wilmington isn't that close to Braxton. It's in North Carolina."

"At least they have good golf courses down there," Daniels said.

"Big deal," snapped Bones McKinney, their 6-6 bassist who three times had bumped his head on one of Schwartzman's low-hanging replica gold records, "nobody in the damn band plays golf."

Bones was clearly upset because his pronounced cowlick was standing even taller than usual and his gigantic Adam's apple was bobbing like it was at a Halloween party.

"When do the recording sessions start?" asked Ashley.

"Well, as soon as the studio is available," said Schwartzman, whose cheeks were starting to flush. "It had been closed for renovations and we had you guys booked for this coming Monday. But there has been a complication. The Prairie Dogs suddenly decided to put out a second album since their first album went platinum. But their sessions shouldn't last long.

You know country music. All their damn songs sound alike so it doesn't take long to record that shit. No creativity needed."

"How long will be the delay?" asked Daniels, thinking about that trial in Braxton.

"About, well, a month," said Schwartzman, softly.

"Fucking great!" yelled Toad, his load of sarcasm dripping from his chin.

"You guys do have money coming in from the record label and the production company, so you won't starve out here," Schwartzman said. "Get settled here in L.A., do some sightseeing, and rehearse your ass off."

"Time is on our side," Daniels said. "Let's make the best of it and let Cy do his job. You guys need some time to find places to live anyway."

Ashley looked at Daniels and saw through his eyes right into his brain box whirring, which had her stomach stirring. She just *knew* that the delay was tempting Daniels to try to pursue his lifelong dream and his trial of a lifetime.

Daniels looked back at Ashley and just *knew* that she knew what he was thinking.

Ashley couldn't wait to get Daniels alone and tell him that he was Cuckoo's Nest insane for even considering balancing the music and trial. She was disappointed that the law had such a hypnotic hold on him.

Daniels couldn't wait to get Ashley alone to tell her why that this delay could not only enable him to pull off his Coffeemate and trial responsibilities, but do so in a way that would keep the band relevant. Listening to Schwartzman, he could already sense that Coffeemate, now that the big media splash was ebbing into the mists of history, would be reduced to being just a glorified cover band. He was more convinced than ever that his lawyering gave Coffeemate its unique clout and identity.

The key was to convince her and the band that he just wasn't trying to have his cake and eat it, too. After all, he had been born without a sweet tooth. History's only recorded sweet virgin birth.

Chapter 15

The Hotel California, otherwise known as the house that Daniels was renting and came with Ashley and the band as house guests, is not what the Eagles sang about. Daniels and Ashley couldn't wait for them to move out and give them some privacy. Of course, Ashley feared the boys would never move out and that she would have to murder all of them. She figured that would give Daniels a high-profile trial in L.A. that would help sell concert tickets. That was contingent about her killing them before Daniels did. Of course, with all dead band members and their vocalist's girlfriend in prison, that would put a definite crimp in their tour.

Beyond the normal invasion of privacy was the reality that the four guys were better suited to be sharing living quarters with the baboons at the Los Angeles Zoo. Their trash seemed to multiply like driver ants.

Pudge spent all of his time farting with more percussion than he displayed on the drums. He sounded like a convoy of tractor-trailers backfiring. And smelled worse than the L.A. sewer system.

Ziggy snored so loudly that it resonated all the way to San Diego and sometimes, on a clear night, all the way to Mexico City.

Bones was clumsier than an elephant on roller skates while drunk on Jack Daniels. Bones never met a glass or dish that he didn't drop and shatter. The Venus di Milo was born with better hands. He did more damage to china than a 5.0 earthquake on the Richter scale. Ashley even went out and bought paper cups and dishes to reduce the carnage.

Toad, who hated to walk even a block while awake, was a chronic sleep-walker who seemed to have a GPS that kept leading him inside Daniels and Ashley's bedroom -- which unfortunately had a broken lock on the door. Once Toad walked in on them in mid-climax for Ashley, who immediately screamed that if Toad wasn't going she was never coming there again. Fortunately, Toad slept through the whole thing and had no clue what he had intruded upon. Thereafter Ashley swore off sex in the house while the band lived there, which didn't please Daniels at all.

Granted, with so little privacy, their sexless bed time afforded the couple more time for pillow talk. Where Daniels gradually and casually began planting the seed, so to speak, over several nights that it was in the band's and all their best marketing interests if he expanded his legal profile by taking the murder trial while their tour and recording sessions were delayed.

"Fuck it," Ashley snapped to Daniels in bed one night or actually 3 in the morning, "do the damn trial. You simply can't resist. So run yourself into the ground being bicoastal working on the trial and rehearsing here with the band to get ready for the tour and studio sessions. Perhaps the delays have been a godsend for you. But you had better not fuck up either the trial or the band because you are spreading yourself thinner than Mexican toilet paper."

"Darling, I love you about a dozen exits past infinity," Daniels gushed through a smile big enough to swallow the Hollywood Hills. Then he laughed and quickly added: "Could you please explain to the band why the trial is a great marketing opportunity for the upcoming tour and album?"

"If you prefer having your penis attached to your body, you will withdraw that question, counselor!" Ashley giggled while smacking Daniels' tousled hair with a pillow.

"Withdrawn," Daniels responded. "Actually, I am going to sell Cy Schwartzman on me doing the trial and then let him sell the band on it. I know that Schwartzman will love the marketing opportunities and will maximize all the conventional media, tabloid media and social media outlets."

The next day Daniels had lunch with Schwartzman in a glitzy Beverly Hills eatery where the prices were only exceeded in size by the implanted boobs of the starlets there to be seen by producers, directors and publicity agents.

Schwartzman was all in immediately.

"You make sure you rehearse your ass off with the band AND be the superstar criminal defense attorney in your little town's crime of the century, and I guarantee you a media circus to make your concert tour and CD blockbusters," Schwartzman said with a huge cigar and slice of filet mignon in his mouth.

"Just don't send in the clowns," Daniels said with his trial face on. "This is a murder trial."

"Don't you worry," Schwartzman said. "I am professional, not a huckster."

"You said that with a straight face," responded Daniels. "Were you an actor at one time?"

"Everybody's an actor in this town," smiled Schwartzman.

That evening Daniels told Ashley and his band that they were meeting with Schwartzman the next morning and it was important.

"He isn't canceling the damn tour and recording session, is he?" asked Pudge, his massive face covered in a massive scowl.

"I knew things were dragging on too slowly," Toad said. "We're getting stale."

"First of all, they are not canceling the tour or the recording session," Daniels assured them. "So relax. He wants to talk about some marketing concepts to help us stay relevant while we wait to tour and record. In the interim, we have to rehearse hard, work on our fresh material to supplement The Doors' covers, and hone our chops."

"Listen to the man," chimed in a smiling Ziggy.

"I'm the man of this band," snapped Toad.

"Of course you are," Daniels said. "I never was into management. Especially middle management where you get shit from the top and the bottom. Management isn't all brass rails and roses."

Chapter 16

Schwartzman's smile was blinding when he sat down -- 15 minutes late -- to discuss Coffeemate's future with the band and Ashley.

"OK, boys, I know you all are more frustrated than a teen-ager dating a virgin, but never fear, Cy is here. There is nothing new on the recording sessions' delay but I have booked a couple dates for you here in the L.A. area, hot clubs where you can knock the rust off performing in front of a live audience and hopefully try out your new original material. As I see it, The Doors' covers are your staple but you must evolve into something more than just a great cover band with an attorney lead singer. That there is just a novelty act.

"That being said," he paused to take a drink of water, "you are blessed with talent. The band plays remarkable music for what started as a bar band from Braxton, PA. And Daniels *is* Jim Morrison when he sings, plus he has that lawyer celeb image. But celebrity is fleeting. 15 minutes of fame is more like 10, unless you get a reality show. By the way, I'm working on that for you. I haven't forgotten you guys. Anyway, we have an extraordinary opportunity to kill two birds with one stone here."

"Get to the point, man," Toad barked.

Cy's smile never waned even one iota.

"Here it is," he said calmly. "While you prep for your recording sessions and start performing live here and at the other limited tour dates that will commence shortly, your buddy Daniels is going to be working his ass off with you and doing the murder trial of this and the last century in your hometown. Daniels is going to realize his dream of handling that trial and use that to help him and all of you realize your dream of stardom in the music world. I will ensure that Daniels' trial gets national media exposure and that marketing will help book a number of touring dates and provide plenty of buzz for your debut album."

"I'm not being totally selfish here," Daniels interjected. "Yes, I want this trial like my next breath and I already talked to the defendant's father and he's happier than a pig in shit to have me lead his defense team, even if it's late coming out of the chute. But I equally want this to work for all of us, to capitalize on my day job to help transform our band into a lucrative day and night job. This will be my final legal defense. But I can't turn this down, and I am thrilled that we can use the trial as leverage to promote us to a greater degree."

"You gonna be here enough to rehearse with us?" Toad challenged.

"Damn right. And I'll also fly all of you home at my expense a couple times so we can rehearse there while I'm moonlighting with the trial. I can pull this off. But I need your support and your faith in me."

"What choice do we have, dude? asked Pudge. "It's already a done deal. But what the fuck? Sounds like a helluva deal for us, too."

"As long as an old fart like you doesn't have a heart attack trying to pull all this off," cracked Ziggy, with a giggle.

"I'm in," Bones said.

"I just wish we were consulted first," Toad said. "Especially me. I'm the goddamn band leader."

"Maybe I copped out, but I thought that it would be better if you heard it from Cy," said Daniels.

"Boys, to be blunt, the reason you are here simply is because of Daniels," chimed in Cy. "He has the voice. He's the hotshot lawyer. Ride this horse until he drops. But just know this, too. The rest of you are much more than a cover band. You can play your asses off. But Daniels is the straw that stirs the drink. The lead vocalist usually is. But he hasn't the time or the interest in being the band leader. He's already told me henceforth that Toad is the band leader and the point person I am to deal with concerning business."

"I can live with that," Toad said. "Thanks, Cy."

"The only person who gets screwed in this is me," Ashley said, with a laugh. "Daniels won't have any time to screw me. But when we make it big, all you other fuckers can move out of our house!"

"You'll miss my cooking," Pudge said loudly through a gap-toothed smile.

"Yeah, I just adore pork chops for breakfast," Ashley said through a smile where all the teeth were lined up like ivory soldiers in perfect formation.

"Guys, from here on I am straddling two worlds and trying not to get my nuts -- or yours -- knocked off in the process," said Daniels, quickly shifting to a more serious tone. "Give me an hour to make some phone calls regarding the trial; then let's rehearse some of our new originals before I segue back to my legal work."

"This all hinges on you, my man," said Toad, rather sternly. "You need to be a superstar in two universes. For the rest of us, being stars in one universe is more than enough. You bit off all this ... damn make sure you can chew it all. I don't give a damn about that kid on trial. But I do give a damn about this band. And if this trial does give our band some more marketing muscle to kick off the tour and album, I'll be the first to kiss your ass."

Daniels looked at Toad and smiled.

"You are absolutely right, Toad. Just know, I care deeply about all of you. You opened up a whole new world for me. It's just that I can't yet turn my back on my old world, especially with this murder trial, which I truly know will create a real buzz for Coffeemate and bring closure to my legal career. Then you all will be seeing so much of me you will be fucking sick of me."

"Nice closing argument, counselor," cracked Bones.

The counselor was acutely aware of what an awesome responsibility he had to his band mates. You only get a single roll of the dice in the music game and if you blow it, you disappear like morning dew.

But Daniels did his best work when a sense of dread rose like summer heat off two-lane blacktop.

Chapter 17

Coffeemate had three really hot sessions in two days working on their new original material -- then all flew back to Braxton, on Daniels' nickel.

The flight was uneventful except for Pudge being strip-searched. The guy strip-searching him was so disgusted by the sight of Pudge naked that he puked right on him. Pudge was not pleased. So he screamed at the poor guy and left the grossest fart. Fortunately, it didn't get any uglier than that.

Back in Braxton, the band partied with their friends and relatives. They drank so much beer that when Bones went to give a pint of blood, they had to blow the head off of it.

Ashley, meanwhile, visited family, and Daniels immersed himself in the trial prep. The first thing Daniels did was meet with Mayor Albert Swanson and the other attorney representing Swanson's son Robert, better known as Biff.

Al Swanson was so excited to see Daniels he almost wet his pants.

Suffice it to say that Douglas Fairbanks, the other attorney, wasn't quite as excited.

Douglas Fairbanks, unlike his Hollywood namesake of long ago, was neither handsome nor dashing. He hardly was a swashbuckling leading man ready to portray Robin Hood or Zorro. This Fairbanks was squat, bald and a Friar Tuck lookalike in his late 30s. His face was so rough it should have been garnished with a lemon slice. He was prone to sweat through his too-small suits that squeezed him like a sausage. And he had chronic bad breath. But he was extremely smart, a zealot, a workaholic and ambitious as hell.

Right away Daniels sensed that the Swanson defense team would not be one awash in harmony. Daniels instantly could tell that Fairbanks wanted to handle the case alone and use the trial to make him the top criminal defense attorney in town, the guy to fill the vacuum left by his departure to the world of rock.

Then things immediately got worse.

"Al tells me that we will be co-lead attorneys on this case and I'm not sure that is going to work," Fairbanks bluntly said almost two minutes after they all said hello. "I told Al that since I have been on Biff's team since they canned that dumb public defender and you were off playing music, I should take the lead and you can offer counsel in the background. You do have years of expertise that I can use to supplement my legal skills."

Swanson almost swallowed his cigar. A cigar that Daniels either wanted to jam up Swanson's ass, then remove and jam into Fairbanks' mouth.

Daniels smiled, his exterior exuding charm and calm while his interior boiled over like a tea kettle. But Daniels never lost his cocksure confidence and his swagger under fire.

"Albert, Albert, Albert, you naughty boy," Daniels said while shaking a finger in the mayor's face. "Tell Mr. Fairbanks here the truth: I am most definitely the lead attorney here. I value Doug's presence on the team and I think it's essential to have two attorneys in a trial of this scope and magnitude. Compounded by my unique situation where I am straddling two distinctly different professional responsibilities. But make no mistake. I am very committed to this case."

Swanson started coughing an apology but Daniels cut him off and decisively stared Fairbanks in his fat face.

"I know you are smart and a real bulldog," Daniels said to him. "That's great. But I will review your work thus far and then you and I will draw up our legal strategy as we develop the case together. Just know that when we disagree on approach, I will listen to your opinion. But ultimately I will orchestrate this, and the baton is in my hand. If you don't accept the deal, you're out."

Daniels then wheeled his attention back to Swanson and snapped: "If either you or Fairbanks gives me any shit over this, I walk. But ask yourself: Is that in the best interests of your son? Actually I'll answer that for you: Fuck no!"

Swanson looked more sheepish than, well, a lamb lying down next to a lion.

"You're right, John," Swanson blustered between nervous coughs. "I should have not used the term co-counsel to Doug. I wanted to soften the blow of you coming on board because I know he wanted to do this by himself. But you are the star in town and I want to hitch my son's fate to your star. That being said, I think Doug is vital to this case with John also engaged in his burgeoning musical career. So both of you please stay on, you guys learn to work together, and get my son off. And learn to work together quickly. There is little time. And, yes, Daniels is the lead dog on this hunt for justice."

Fairbanks said nothing for almost two minutes. He already knew that he would work under Daniels' terms because he couldn't walk away from all the publicity. He needed to leverage that to expand his career once Daniels was totally into music. But he wanted to make both Daniels and Swanson sweat for a couple minutes. He liked to make other people sweat since he himself was a walking sprinkler system in a suit.

"Understood," Fairbanks finally said. "You should have been straight up with me from the beginning, Albert. But this is too important of a case to walk away from. I respect your vast experience, Daniels, and I will abide by your wishes. But I strongly will offer my input and hopefully two heads are better than one."

"With our egos, we both have big heads," Daniels laughed, breaking the tension. "As long as the defense table is wide enough in the courtroom, we can make this work."

Daniels lied. On the way to Miller County Prison to meet Biff Swanson for the first time Daniels was regretting taking the case. He was livid at Al Swanson for lying to him. And he sensed a lot of interference from Fairbanks. This trial already was compromised by Daniels' divided attention and he was so hoping for a supportive attorney to work with him. He wished he had known more about Fairbanks before taking this case. The case had become more frustrating than being a blind Peeping Tom. Now Daniels knew that Fairbanks wasn't the right guy for the job.

"He has to be screwed up with a name like that," Daniels said to his steering wheel in a quick exhale of gallows humor.

If Daniels was deeply worried that a botched Swanson case would be disaster for his Braxton legacy, he was gravely scared shitless that was the case when he met Biff.

Robert Swanson truly was a Biff. He looked like he had just fallen off a surfboard. He was a 6-2, 185-pound former high school jock – all blond hair and broad shoulders. He was laid back to the point of being comatose at times. At other times he could be more animated than a cartoon character on crank. He was cocky and arrogant, with absolutely no respect for authority. He had a sense of entitlement large enough to require a three-car garage.

Worse, Daniels soon discovered that Biff didn't seem to be that concerned with the fine details, like working with his legal team. Biff told Daniels that he was confident that his old man's stature would get him off. Biff thought he could skate by this, just like he had skated or surfed by everything else in life. For a kid who told his dad that he was scared shitless, he sure as hell didn't act the part.

All this was telescoped into the first few minutes of Daniels' opening conservation with Biff Swanson.

"Robert, I'm John Daniels, your lead defense attorney."

Which elicited a yawn from Biff and no eye contact. Finally, he simply said: "Call me Biff, dude."

Which drew an immediate rebuke from Daniels.

"The name is John Daniels. I am not a dude. I'm the guy who can help save your ass in what is an extremely important matter. You are accused of raping and murdering a 17-year-old girl who was the daughter of the city police chief. The bastard who did that has to be the dumbest fuck in the world. You don't realize how much heat is on your ass for being accused of this heinous crime."

"Chill, man," Biff said through a sliver of a smile and with his eyes still looking down at his fingernails as if they were the most fascinating objects in the known universe. "Oops. Daniels. Yeah, I know this is sort of serious shit. But hey, I'm innocent. It's your job to prove that. That's what my old man is paying you for. What do you want me to fucking do?"

"Help me save your ass, asshole!" Daniels barked with menace. "You have to give me your undivided cooperation and attention. You do what I say. You act like I say. Everything you do in the courtroom has to convince the jury you're innocent as a lamb, a choirboy who wouldn't swat a fly -- not some punk thug who raped a young girl so violently that her vagina was torn and then choked the last breath out of her by almost snapping her neck off. You act like you just did with me and the jury will be convinced you're such an animal and fry your ass! Got that, Biff baby?"

For the first time Biff not only looked Daniels in the face, but stared into his eyes. Biff Swanson showed no emotion, no fear, no remorse, no nothing. He was more detached than a poor prizefighter's retina.

He said just one word: "Whatever!"

Daniels bored a hole into Biff's unseeing eyes. "I'll be back tomorrow to see you," Daniels said calmly. "You had better have an attitude adjustment by then. You're facing a first-degree murder charge. Think about that overnight, pretty boy. Then decide whether you should smarten up immediately or risk death row or life behind bars and be catnip for all those sexual predators in prison.

"One final thing: The victim was the daughter of Fred Driscoll, the police chief of Braxton. A guy your old man just fired. And the DA is Big Jim Gallagher, a former state cop. You think those guys don't want to burn your ass? You need me like you need your next breath!"

Biff finally blinked. And Daniels thought he saw a slight gulp as well.

When Daniels walked out of the prison, one compelling thought walked in tandem with him: I left the music world in L.A. for the pure joy of wrestling with Biff Swanson, Douglas Fairbanks and Big Jim Gallagher, a DA who went for the jugular with every ounce of his 275-pound frame.

"I must be the dumb fuck," Daniels said aloud.

Chapter 18

The next morning Daniels met with Fairbanks to review the evidence. It gave Daniels a mixed picture and a ray of hope.

The key DNA evidence in a rape/murder by strangulation trial invariably comes in the form of semen and hairs collected at the crime scene. Sweat, skin, hair, blood and saliva also leave DNA fingerprints.

It appeared that Biff Swanson left his DNA all over and inside pretty and petite Danielle Driscoll.

"That's going to be tough to refute," Fairbanks said, apparently reluctant to wield a swashbuckling sword in his defense approach.

"Yes and no," Daniels said confidently.

"You don't think they sort of have Swanson dead to rights?" asked Fairbanks.

"They probably do," Daniels replied calmly. "After meeting Swanson yesterday, and without profiling him, I definitely think he may have done it. That is not my concern. Our job is to get him off, to give him the best defense possible. Cut and dried. If the prosecution has a case sealed tight, they will win. And justice will be served.

"But how do we know that? Perhaps the semen was somehow compromised. That would make it inconclusive whether it belongs to Biff. And could the semen have been planted on her and inside her? The same goes for the hair on her. After all, the girl was the daughter of the police chief, a man feuding with a mayor who was ready to blow the whistle on him and blow away his career and eventually did just that. Anything is possible, including implicating the mayor's punk son as the rapist/killer."

"Do you really think the DA would be a party to that? And do you really believe that the then chief and the Braxton cops would be capable of that?" asked Fairbanks, his eyes bigger than silver dollars on growth hormones.

"Maybe, maybe not," Daniels said. "But we have to at least create that doubt in the jury. I have an expert on call from New York who is the Sherlock Holmes of DNA detective work. Was there any sloppy police work with the DNA? Or was it intentionally planted or altered? Were there any contamination or storage issues?

"Biff was previously arrested by the Braxton police for hitting a guy and breaking a window at The Juicy Oyster. They already had samples of Swanson's DNA. Perhaps they planted that DNA at the rape/murder scene. Those paper towels with Swanson's DNA that the cops say they found at the crime scene, claiming Biff used them to wipe his penis after the rape? Easy to plant, I say. And if a guy like Biff just raped and choked a girl to death, do you think he would worry about a little cum on his cock? And if so, would he be stupid enough to wipe cum off his cock with paper towels and leave them just lying there on the girl's stomach?

"Let's make sure we float plenty of clouds of doubt in front of the jury."

"What are you turning this trial into?" asked Fairbanks.

"We are going to turn Biff's rape/murder trial into a trial of the Braxton police department. Simple as that. But it is going to be a tremendous amount of work. We must challenge every single piece of evidence that the prosecution enters. We have to do a masterful job in handling the DNA evidence. We have to outclass the prosecution. We will do exactly what the defense is supposed to do. Find every hole in the prosecution's case. The jury will respond to that.

"Our defense essentially is to convince each jury member that they can't trust the messenger because the messenger has lied to them, and that means that the jury members can't trust the message the prosecution is presenting to them. So if you have police officers that are lying to the jury, that aren't testifying to them truthfully, there's no reason for the jury to believe that all of the physical evidence that the prosecution collected and presented is as reliable as it suggests. There's reason for the jury to fear incompetence and worse: corruption of the physical evidence. And then the jury certainly can't trust the story the prosecution is telling about Biff in this case."

"Oh my God!" exclaimed Fairbanks, looking aghast. "Criminal defense attorneys must have a fidelity to the judicial system itself. We must observe that."

Daniels smiled and said softly: "We do? The culture of criminal courtrooms is this: The fundamental ethic for a criminal defense lawyer is to do anything he can to get his client off, and it's up to the system to restrain the criminal defense attorney. And when that system of restraint is relaxed, a defense lawyer runs wild."

"I'm not sure I can be a party to this travesty," Fairbanks huffed and puffed.

"Then quit," Daniels barked. "Listen, Biff Swanson is an asshole. He can't help it. It's in his DNA. If he is a punk on the witness stand, and I believe he will be, we will turn that into our advantage. We will convince the jury that the police chief was so blinded by the rage he feels for the mayor and by his mourning over his daughter's rape and murder that, with no other suspects, he pounced on a jerkoff like Biff to be the sacrificial lamb and wreak vengeance on the mayor. The mayor's charges that Fred Driscoll is a crooked cop are icing on our cake."

"You're fucking insane!" Fairbanks shouted, walking away with a derisive snort.

But Daniels knew that that they would only get one shot at defusing this nuclear missile.

"We do it my way or Biff doesn't have a fucking chance," Daniels shouted at Fairbanks' back. "When I tell Albert Swanson, do you think he's going to side with you or me? He's already told the media that the police planted evidence to frame his son. All we are doing is convincing the jury that Al Swanson is right."

Daniels spent the remainder of the day and early evening reviewing the DNA evidence and talking on the phone several times with his forensic DNA expert in Manhattan. Dr. Morton Anderson III could break down DNA as if he had a bionic brain, bionic eyes and bionic equipment. He was the best in the business and he didn't come cheap.

"I will be in town tomorrow," Dr. Anderson told Daniels, "considering the late start you are giving me on this. Can your client afford me?"

"Doubtful," Daniels said. "I will help with your expenses and retainer. And you will negotiate a discount with me because, trust me, this case is going to be so high profile that you will spend every waking minute of the rest of your life in the lab or in a courtroom."

"So how will that change my life?" asked Dr. Anderson. "I already do. Book me somewhere nice for three days to start."

"The Homewood Plaza is the best I can do for you," Biff said. "It's not the Ritz but I'll buy you a great dinner at The Nut Bar tomorrow night."

The problem was that not only did Dr. Anderson arrive in town the next day and began his DNA exploration and did indeed have dinner with Daniels. Actually, that wasn't the problem. Daniels was supposed to rehearse with the band that night and totally blew off the gig.

Not a good move, counselor.

At 10 p.m. that night Toad called Daniels and said they would look for a new lead singer if it happened again. Daniels was going to apologize, but got pissed himself and simply wished Toad good luck with that. Which got Toad angrier than a hornet being sprayed with mace.

At 10:22 p.m. Pudge called Daniels and said he would break every bone in his body twice if it happened again. Daniels simply told Pudge to calm down and eat more salads. To which Pudge cleverly retorted, "Go fuck yourself."

At 10:33 p.m. Ziggy called Daniels and merely sobbed uncontrollably. Daniels offered to send him a box of Kleenex.

At 10:49 p.m. Bones called Daniels to tell him that he understood and knew he was committed to Coffeemate and it had been an honest oversight. Daniels replied, "Bones, you're smarter than the others. Tell them I'm no asshole and I will make this up to them."

Bones replied, "I'm not that stupid."

The ensuing night Daniels forgot about his dinner date with Ashley and instead dined with Dr. Anderson once again, this time at Dante's Restaurant. When Daniels arrived home at 9:30, he found two things: One, his underwear was strewn all over the front lawn. Two, Ashley had eaten a peanut butter and jelly sandwich for dinner in his absence. She didn't tell him this because she had texted him she would never speak to him again in this life. Daniels deduced what Ashley had for dinner because peanut butter and jelly and bread crumbs were smeared all over his side of the bed.

Daniels smiled at the sullen Ashley and said: "Actually, I find sleeping on my family room recliner to be quite comfortable." In response, Ashley sent Daniels the following text: "I just had my cousin pick it up for his rec room."

"I must say that the band and you have slightly overreacted, like trying to kill a fly with a machine gun," Daniels said softly.

The hurt and loss of his favorite recliner were still new and hot to the touch.

Chapter 19

For three days Ashley refused to speak to Daniels. And she hardly was wearing the skin off her pretty fingers from texting him. She sent just two texts. One said: "You suck!" The other said: "Fuck you!"

A whole cavalcade of emotion spilled through her system, but mostly anger settled over her like a shroud while a sickly pale gray gloom dulled her soul.

Daniels was very remorseful and in contrast, kept texting whole chapters to Ashley – pleading for her to forgive him, to please understand the stresses he was enduring while balancing two all-consuming pursuits, to realize that both endeavors were extremely important to both of them, and to also realize that this massive time commitment was short-term.

When Daniels wasn't texting, he was immersed in trial preparation and band rehearsals. The band members were distant from him to a degree. He hardly had time to sleep. And when he did, it was on an air mattress he had just purchased and put in one of the other bedrooms.

When Daniels decided a large part of his case hinged on discrediting the DNA evidence even though he had no preliminary evidence of that, he was confident that someone as skilled as Dr. Morton Anderson III could discover something amiss in the lab results.

It was common for cases involving even less serious crimes to be solved with DNA evidence in the everyday world of Miller County investigations. With more local departments than ever submitting material, there often was a huge backlog in getting lab results. Granted, there was a faster response involving violent crimes against people. But nobody ever would dare describe it as warp speed.

The key was for Dr. Anderson to play detective as if he were Sherlock Holmes on steroids and find errors made during control tests. The whole point was to create doubt about the DNA evidence in the minds of the jury.

Complicating matters, the prosecution knew that Anderson worked with Daniels. So they refused to make the DNA evidence available to the defense for its own testing to make it more difficult for Anderson and Daniels to uncover any bungling by police technicians handling the samples. So Anderson would have to do his own testing in a limited time period.

Another key was for Daniels to uncover any hint of evidence planted by cops out to crucify the mayor and his son because of Swanson's feud with their now former chief.

Needless to say, John Daniels hardly had the time for Jack Daniels/Jim Morrison, let alone Ashley. But he knew he had to make the time for Ashley and Coffeemate. Since both she and his band wanted to strangle him with guitar string, he knew he had to make quality time for both. After a 10-hour day working on the trial, Daniels had a jamming two-hour rehearsal with the band and everybody said afterwards that their chops on their 10 new original songs were better than ever. Suddenly they were treating him once again as one of their own.

He committed to another rehearsal in two nights. The next night was reserved for Ashley, unless she had run off with their mailman by then. After all, she had been going pretty postal on Daniels lately. When he got home after the band session, he prayed that Ashley would be at home and not in a mood to stab two steak knives into his eyes. After all, he didn't have time to learn Braille so he could review all of Doc Anderson's DNA reports.

Fortunately, Ashley was empty-handed when he walked in the family room. And fortunately Daniels was not empty-handed. In one hand he had a dozen red roses. In the other he had a customized sympathy card in which he had altered the language on the cover to read: *My condolences on the passing of your asshole boyfriend. May he rest in hell.*

He handed the roses to her, which she promptly threw on the floor and snapped: "Considering your damn neglect, it should have been two dozen."

"The entire floral shop inventory will be here tomorrow by noon," Daniels quickly retorted, fighting desperately and creatively for his romantic life. "It would have been here already but their delivery truck broke down."

For a second a flicker of a smile surfaced on Ashley's lovely face. But she quickly caught herself and turned that brief smile upside down like a blitzing linebacker sacking a quarterback.

Daniels decided to hold up the card instead of handing it to her. When he did so, she simply couldn't help herself. She laughed and then screamed: "I fucking hate you, Daniels!"

He then tossed the card on the coffee table, gently pulled her toward him and gave here the sweetest kiss of his or her life. At first he needed the Jaws of Life to pry open her lips enough to even glimpse her tongue. Two minutes later their tongues were wrestling like two alligators in Everglades heat.

After their kiss, Ashley pulled away and calmly said: "Of course, this changes nothing. How the hell are you going to squeeze me into your life? Will this double life as attorney and rock singer end with this trial? Or will another juicy murder trial lure you? Will you ever find the time to be my husband and the father of my children?"

You could have knocked Daniels over with a strand of dental floss. It had been the first time that Ashley had ever mentioned marriage and children. He had mentioned both a few times earlier in their relationship, only to be dismissed by

Ashley's disclaimer that "I'm sure as hell not the marrying kind and I would suck as a mother."

Tears welled in Daniels eyes. Upon seeing his eyes, tears welled in Ashley's eyes. While their respecting water levels were rising, both stood there in solemn silence for several moments. They both realized that this was a transcendent moment in their lives, that neither they nor their relationship would ever be the same moments from THE moment. Their relationship would either evolve or devolve. The status quo suddenly was as extinct as a dinosaur rock guitarist.

Ashley waited for Daniels to make the next move. She was so nervous that she had to press her feet into the carpet to keep her knees from knocking like bongo drums. She somewhat expected him to suddenly grin like the conquering man and try to squire her to bed to begin the reproductive process. And if he tried to do so, she expected that she would bail on the relationship but she wasn't certain because his hypnotic hold on her was that strong.

Daniels had no intention of doing so. He was a man of depth and he had an acute sense of the gravity of the moment. He reverently and slowly dropped to one knee and said:

"Ashley, I solemnly promise that this absolutely will be my last trial in Braxton. That henceforth I will be primarily devoted to you and secondarily devoted to my musical career. Most importantly, will you marry me?"

She clasped her face in her hands and began sobbing and squealing -- making a sound that startled her and added 20 years of current to Daniels' heart.

"Oh my God, yes! Yes!"

Daniels quickly arose and gave her a kiss and hug that was a delicious blend of tenderness and passion.

When their lips finally parted, Daniels softly asked, "Can I escort my future wife to dinner?"

She smiled and simply said, "Sweet."

Their dinner at an upscale restaurant was sweet. And that had nothing to do with their sweet cuisine.

Of course, Ashley was the type who got quickly bored with sweetness.

On the drive home she started tongue-in-cheek conversation on why the world was a better place when everybody smoked cigarettes. She then proceeded to stick an unlit Marlboro in each of Daniels' nostrils, who almost drove off the road.

Chapter 20

Daniels was sitting in his office, drinking his morning coffee while reviewing some of Doc Anderson's DNA reports that indicated perhaps the Braxton police force may have been sloppier than a truck stop waitress with some of the samples.

The phone rang and when Daniels heard what Braxton mayor Al Swanson screamed in his ear, he slammed down his coffee cup and spilled hot coffee on his crotch.

"Damn it!" Daniels bellowed at both his crotch and Swanson.

"Look, John, this is my kid and his ass is on the line," Swanson snapped back. "Don't scream at me. I'm paying you good money to save Biff's ass, not to play The Music Man. Douglas Fairbanks tells me that he thinks you're distracted by your music and not paying attention to the case. You are bicoastal right now, so that's why I gave Douglas the green light to run the show."

At that moment Daniels considered Swanson and Fairbanks to be in a dead heat for the most hated man in America, by a par 5.

"Stick that green light up your ass and you'll see that your brains are in your ass," Daniels said sternly. "I run the show or I'm out. Doc Anderson and I are focused as hell on this trial and we think we have a great defense in attacking the DNA evidence. Your cops just may be as dirty as you think. And sloppier than you think. Fairbanks thinks I'm nuts. Go with his cookie-cutter defense and Biff will never walk the streets again. Your call."

Swanson started muttering, swearing, stammering and blustering.

"Look asshole!" Daniels barked. "We have to defuse this damn time bomb. David Copperfield tried to make 747s disappear. I'm going to try to defend your son. Let me work my magic."

"OK, I'll tell Fairbanks you're back on top!" Swanson finally spit out with a snake's tongue.

"Not good enough!" barked back Daniels. "Fire his ass! I can get more done without his interference. He's the distraction, not my music career."

"I can't do that quite yet," Swanson said. "Wouldn't be right. But if he balks at your return to lead dog, I will terminate his services."

"When the hell did you start worrying about what's right?" jabbed Daniels.

"I'll forget you said that, John."

Five minutes after Daniels finished with Swanson, Cy Schwartzman, their agent, called with great news for Coffeemate and terrible news for Daniels' stress levels.

"Cy, it's 5:30 in the morning on the West Coast," Daniels said. "Did you just get in from a night of drinking?"

"Very funny, counselor," coughed Schwartzman. "I need you guys out here. Now! The Prairie Dogs cut short their recording sessions and you can now get to work on your album. Their lead singer was busted for a DUI. He was naked as a jaybird in the car. And now he's in rehab. When he gets out, their tour dates will sell out. People love singers who are a mess. Also, I've booked some early tour dates faster than I anticipated. That's why I get up early. I get things done."

Schwartzman had made a fortune representing contemporary artists even though he longed for the days when popular songs had melodies, and the lyrics didn't say it was a good idea to murder mom and dad or the police.

And he got up early to get things done because he spent most afternoons playing golf, a hacker who owned a tee ball that could pretty much imitate a boomerang in flight.

Daniels was part thrilled and a whole lot torn over Schwartzman's news.

"We will be back in L.A. as soon as possible," Daniels said. "I still have to balance the music with the trial, though."

"You're nuts," Schwartzman said. "But I will parlay the publicity I generate from the trial to hype the CD and tour. How's the trial prep going?"

"Great," Daniels said. "Working on a great defense. Also have filed for an extension on the trial date because of all the evidence we are reviewing. I'm hoping the trial doesn't start for at least two months."

"Tough to schedule concerts around a trial when I don't know the start date," Schwartzman said. "Even I'm not that good. But at least you can get the album finished and do some tour dates. When can you be in L.A.?"

"In two days," Daniels said, wondering how the hell that miracle was going to break a sweat.

"Tomorrow's better," Schwartzman said.

"Talk to you later, Cy."

Daniels then let out a sigh that could have propelled Columbus from the Old World to the New World and back again.

He quickly called Ashley and asked her to call all the band members to alert them they were returning to L.A. in two days.

"Great," gushed Ashley. "Let's hear the music. You can still do your legal research in L.A. That's why they invented laptops, iPads and smartphones."

"Let me know when they invent the 48-hour day," Daniels said with a flicker of gallows humor. "I got a real busy day and tomorrow ahead of me, hon. I know you understand."

"You're cruising for a heart attack, babe," she scolded. "If that doesn't kill you, I will. Now put your ass to the grindstone."

"It's put your nose to the grindstone."

"I like your nose and I don't want you to mess it up," Ashley parried.

Daniels spent the next few hours reviewing DNA evidence and became more and convinced that the cops and the lab were careless and compromised some of the samples. Late that morning Doc Anderson called him with more animation in his voice than Daniels had ever heard. Normally, Anderson was as animated as a stop sign.

"Daniels, the cops planted some of Biff's DNA at the crime scene," he said with palpable excitement. "It seems too old to belong. I think they took it from one of the kid's prior arrests."

"If you were here, I would kiss you on the lips," Daniels shouted.

"Damn, you'll split my eardrum like a watermelon," complained Anderson.

With a return to L.A. imminent, Daniels decided it was time to fish or cut bait with Douglas Fairbanks even though fishing was never a hobby of his and he had never been in a tackle shop.

Over lunch time he stopped in at a toy store and purchased a pair of plastic swords. He then stopped in unexpectedly at Fairbanks' office on Court Street near the courthouse.

Fairbanks' receptionist looked at Daniels as if he had two heads when she saw him standing there clutching two plastic swords.

"John Daniels here! Is Douglas in?" he asked with a huge smile. "I want to see if the swashbuckling namesake wants to fight me."

Without even a hint of a smile curling across her lips, she buzzed Fairbanks on the intercom and said: "Daniels is here and he apparently wants to sword fight you. Should I send him in?"

"Tell him to go fuck himself," Fairbanks screamed back, immediately transforming his receptionist's face redder than Lenin and Stalin while reading Karl Marx and drinking vodka.

While she was momentarily stunned, Daniels zipped right past her and into Fairbanks' office. A former long jumper in track and still athletic in middle age, Daniels leaped over Fairbanks' desk and made a gymnast's acrobatic landing right next to Fairbanks. The latter couldn't have been more startled had he been awakened by a gorilla.

"You've been fighting me all along on this trial, so let's get as real as two old guys can get with plastic swords in their hands," Daniels shouted and laughed. "Live up to your namesake and cross swords with me since you've been stabbing me in the back with Swanson."

Daniels tossed Fairbanks a sword and the latter instinctively caught it.

"Are you insane?" Fairbanks yelped, still looking spectacularly astonished.

"Don't play games," Daniels said. "I know you've been telling Swanson I can't handle the trial and be a rock star all at the same time. Guess what? I can. But I need your help. You have to buy into my DNA evidence defense and work with Doc Anderson's research while I'm in L.A. I am focused on the trial on either coast, but you need to be more hands-on and have my back."

"Why the hell should I do that?" Fairbanks asked.

"Because playing ball with me will make you a rich man when we win this trial and you are the alpha criminal defense attorney in town because I'm out of here. And because then I won't tip off your wife about your mistress."

It was a good thing that Fairbanks wasn't playing poker at the time because his poker face flashed one big tell of guilt.

"What mistress?" stammered Fairbanks.

"Don't mess with me. Victoria is her name. Your Victoria's secret."

"Your ethics suck and now you are resorting to blackmail, huh?" asked Fairbanks, the anger now flushing his face.

"Precisely, my moral man," Daniels said, punctuated by a wicked laugh. "Now clear your schedule. You're spending all afternoon and evening with me and I am going to convince you that our DNA defense is going to win the day."

Fairbanks, looking like a guy who just had been run over by a John Deere tractor, meekly surrendered and agreed.

Daniels playfully stabbed Fairbanks in the heart with his sword and said, "See you in my office in an hour."

Gulping his seventh cup of coffee of the day, Daniels welcomed Fairbanks into his conference room.

Four hours and three more cups of coffee by Daniels later, Fairbanks evidently had an epiphany.

"I have to admit, and this has nothing to do with Victoria, but I now get this," he said. "This is brilliant. Trust me, you can trust me. I will work my ass off while you have to be in L.A. And we will win this trial."

"Glad to have you on board," Daniels said. "Just don't share any details with anybody. You, Doc and I are the only ones who need to know the specifics of this."

"I understand," Fairbanks said.

When Daniels got home late that night, he kissed Ashley, and immediately sat down, suddenly dizzy, in one of his kitchen chairs. A minute later he passed out and slid off the chair as if it were freshly shellacked and crumpled on the floor.

Ashley let out a scream loud enough to awaken the demons smoking in the dungeons of hell and then called 911. Fifteen minutes later an ambulance crew was lifting Daniels onto a gurney.

Daniels, coming out of his fog, immediately realized what the hell was going on, and loudly protested, "Put me down. I'm OK. Just fainted. I'm dehydrated. Drank too much coffee and not enough water."

"Relax, Mr. Daniels," said one of the EMR technicians, a guy burly enough to fight one of the current half-dozen heavyweight champions of the world. "You may have suffered a heart attack. The hospital will have to run some tests."

"I don't have the time, I'm fine," Daniels said, his temper flaring.

"Don't be insane, Daniels," Ashley interrupted. "You're going! That's it!"

Daniels' serenity was more shattered than a window that went one on one with a thrown rock, totally pissed that destiny had thrown him a left hook right on the kisser.

Chapter 21

Daniels couldn't have been more uncomfortable if someone had jammed a cactus up his ass.

There he was in the Braxton Hospital ER, lying on a bed at 3 a.m. in the morning waiting for more tests in the morning.

"I'm fine, Ashley," he said, a look of high-octane irritation running curl patterns all over his face. "You should have realized that I just passed out."

"I thought you had a heart attack, Jack," she said, trying to keep him calm. "If you were 22, I would have figured you had passed out. But at your age ..."

Daniels jumped on her last word faster than a jungle cat bouncing off a trampoline.

"My age? I ain't that freaking old. Plus, look at me! For a guy who doesn't have time to work out much, I'm a stud. For any age."

"Sure you are Jack," she said, getting somewhat annoyed and sarcastic. "Keep lying to yourself and you could wind up lying in your grave."

Before he could counter, the ER doctor walked in.

"You look like you are about 12," Daniels said to the physician, who actually did despite being 28 years old.

"It's just because you're an old man," chimed in Ashley.

Daniels then fired Ashley a searing look that could have melted the chrome off a '57 Chevy.

"Actually, Mr. Daniels, because of your age we are going to keep you overnight to run more tests tomorrow," said the ER doc. "You likely are just dehydrated but we have to rule out any possible cardiac issues."

"I have to be in L.A. in two days so can we wrap things up tomorrow?" Daniels asked.

"You might have to wait an extra day until the cardiologist has a chance to review the test results," said the kid doc. "Of course, if they find something is wrong, you may have to change your plans."

"That is not an option," Daniels said forcefully.

"Don't be foolish, Jack," scolded Ashley.

"You likely be will check out just fine, so don't get upset until you find out otherwise," reassured the doctor. "Don't want to get your blood pressure up. Good luck and good health."

"Screw this," Daniels said aloud right after the doc left. "I don't have time to be a cardiac patient."

"What's more important here, Jack?" Ashley asked softly. "The trial? The band? Me? Your life?"

"All of the above," Jack said. "I will have it all."

"You're working too damn much," Ashley said.

"This is no fucking time to throttle back on my workload," Jack fired back. "I will be fine. Hell, I AM fine!"

The next day the tests indicated that his heart seemed to be working just fine but of course Daniels had to wait another day to see the cardiologist before being discharged. His patience was wearing thinner than an elite marathoner on a severe diet. Fortunately, his secretary brought him plenty of trial briefs to review to help pass the time and help grease the skids for his L.A. departure.

Two things really had frosted Daniels on his day of tests. One, the guy pushing his gurney around from test to test was about 80 years old and said he had never spent a day in the hospital except to volunteer. Two, his band mates spent the day busting his balls big time – not exactly a charitable thing to do to a potential cardiac patient.

"Just because a heart attack killed Morrison, you don't have to cover that part of him," jabbed Toad.

"Maybe we should change our name to Cardiac Arrest," joked Pudge.

"If anybody is a candidate for a heart attack in this band, it's you Pudge," countered Daniels. "Lay off the bacon cheeseburgers. And for the record, I was just freaking dehydrated."

"Perhaps you should bring six bottles of water on stage for every gig instead of the usual three," said Bones.

"He'll then be taking piss breaks," chimed in Ziggy, normally a pipsqueak.

"Hey, what's got into you, Ziggy?" laughed Daniels. "You used to be the only nice guy in the band."

Just then Pudge exploded with a fart that almost knocked over a skinny nurse who came in to take Daniels' blood pressure.

Pudge wouldn't reveal what he had eaten for dinner that evening, but judging from the reeking stench of that fart, it had to be a diseased yak.

While everyone's eyes still were stinging and Ashley was fanning herself with a towel, in walked Al Swanson to visit Daniels.

Swanson checked out the Coffeemate crew and his sour look of disgust said it all: What the hell was Daniels doing playing with these losers when Biff was in severe jeopardy?

"Hi Al," Daniels said, smiling. "Say hello to these future Grammy winners."

Swanson muttered a guttural "Hello" and even the Coffeemate boys picked up on the cue.

"Well, we gotta get going and jam a little big tonight," Toad said. "The instrumentals are essential, especially when your vocalist could hit the deck at any moment."

"See ya, Hydro Man," cracked Bones. "You too, Mr. Mayor, Your Honor."

"You know, I have to go get some takeout," Ashley said, "since Daniels won't be taking me out to dinner tonight."

She walked over to Daniels' bed and kissed him tenderly on the cheek and said: "Thank God I still have you. I thought you had had a fatal heart attack for a few minutes, babe. You gotta stop working so hard before it kills you."

Ashley and the band then left and left Swanson alone with Daniels. The latter sensed the former didn't come to inquire about his health out of concern, but rather to assess whether Daniels could withstand the rigors of a murder trial.

He was spot on.

"You good enough to handle the trial and this music shit?" Swanson asked sternly. "Seriously, can't you put the music on hold until after the trial? I'll never forgive you if we lose because you squandered time pretending to be a degenerate rocker like Jim Morrison."

"You knew the deal when I signed on," Daniels snapped, his face hardening with anger. "Ninety percent of me is better than 120 percent of any other lawyer you can find. And to be honest, I've been short-changing the band and giving you 110 percent. I realize the gravity of this. I was just dehydrated, that's all. Too much coffee while reviewing the DNA evidence with Fairbanks, who apparently now agrees with my defense strategy. I really think we can win this. So stick with me and don't give me any shit. But if you no longer think we're a fit, I'll quit. You and Biff need me more than I need this trial."

"You're full of shit," Swanson said. "You need this trial like your next breath. We both need each other, as does Biff. I just wanted to make sure you're healthy."

"Healthy as a horse's ass," laughed Daniels.

The next morning Doc Anderson reported for duty in Daniels' private room while the latter waited for the cardiologist to stop by and release him.

Doc and Daniels spent two hours immersed in their research and defense strategy. Files were strewn all over the floor and on Daniels' bed. A 20-something nurse in a rush came in and slipped on some of the paperwork, lost her balance, and fell atop Daniels' lap just as the cardiologist walked in.

"Thank God all your tests and blood work are just fine," said Dr. Oliver Munchak III, a model picture of fitness with sculpted muscles and sleek lines. "Otherwise frolicking with this pretty young nurse in your hospital bed could cause an irregular heartbeat. I'm releasing you immediately for the sake of our nursing staff."

Daniels and the usually stoic Doc Anderson laughed out loud, as did Dr. Munchak. But the nurse, her face flushed crimson red with embarrassment, was a stammering mess.

"I'm so sorry, Doctor, I slipped and fell on the patient. This isn't what it looks like."

"You rock stars sure do get the groupies," Dr. Munchak said, laughing again.

The nurse, who couldn't have looked more startled had she been electrocuted in the shower, looked in disbelief at Daniels and blurted out: "Oh my God, you're a rock star?!"

Daniels flashed a devilish green and proclaimed. "Well, yes. I'm Jim Morrison."

"You are?" squealed the nurse in disbelief. "I thought you WERE dead!"

"I soon will be," Daniels laughed, "since my girlfriend just walked in the room."

The nurse sprang up like a Jill-in-the-box and her face flushed crimson once again at the sight of Ashley, who picked up the cue and played along.

"I've caught you with another groupie, hey? Nurse, do they castrate patients here? Can I help?"

Ashley couldn't control her giggles and the nurse joined in the laughter.

"It's good to laugh," Daniels said as he scurried to get dressed after the medical professionals had left his room. "Great news, Ash. It was only dehydration. So from now on I'm going to drink more water than a damn camel. By the way, I will be home to pack shortly so we can fly to L.A. tomorrow. But first Doc and I have to pay a visit to Biff Swanson."

"Lucky you guys," she said. "He must be a real punk."

"Oh, he is," Daniels said. "I just don't think he's a killer. I know the DNA evidence implicates him strongly, but ol' Doc here thinks we just may something to create doubt about the DNA in the jury's minds. For instance, the semen could have been planted on her and inside her. The same for the hair on her body. Yep, the DNA could have been intentionally planted or altered. And there could have been contamination and storage issues. Busy labs sometimes get sloppy."

"The police did have samples of Biff's DNA from a previous arrest," said Anderson. "And from what I could see, some of the DNA samples seem too dated. But we want to talk to Biff to see if he had any recent sexual relationships with the girl. That would be most helpful."

Doc Anderson and Daniels found Biff to be, well, Biff. He seemed as nonchalant as ever about the severity of a first-degree murder trial. He was aloof and uncooperative, stonewalling for almost 10 minutes of remarkable evasion that was more awkward than an arthritic aardvark with two broken legs.

The highlight, or the lowlight, of that non-conversation came when Daniels angrily vented by his frustration by asking Swanson if he would talk "if I shoved a glass rod in your cock and slapped it around until the glass shatters inside it, would you then answer me?"

"I would be too busy screaming, I guess, to offer an intelligent answer," Swanson said, his smirk bigger than a Hoover attachment.

"I know you aren't a rocket scientist," Daniels countered, "but even a retarded water buffalo couldn't be this dumb. By not cooperating with us, you likely will get convicted of first-degree murder and rape. Meaning either the death penalty or life in prison. I suspect that will mean the same thing for you. A punk pussy like you will get a shiv in the heart from one of the other felons."

That got Biff's attention. He finally locked eyes for a moment with Daniels, then darted a worried glance at Doc Anderson.

"So you want to know if I fucked her with her consent prior to the rape?" Biff finally. "So what if I did? I told her I wouldn't tell anybody. Do you want me to break a promise to a dead lady?"

"OK, so you did have intercourse with her," chimed in Doc Anderson. "How long before the night she was raped and murdered."

"I don't know which night she was raped and murdered," Biff said, smiling. "I wasn't there."

"It was July 14th," snapped Daniels.

"Hell, I don't know," Biff said. "Two, three weeks I guess. We only did it once. She was a lousy lay. Too young, I guess. She was too worried that my condom would break and she would get pregnant or get AIDS. That kind of spoiled the mood, you know what I mean?"

"If we win this case, remind me to rip your head off," Daniels said calmly.

"And I will totally dissect you during the autopsy," Doc Anderson added, which totally was out of character for such a reserved man.

"Do you think I care what you two old fucks think?" Biff asked with a sarcastic laugh.

"I didn't know that horseshit could talk," Daniels said, complete with his own sarcastic laugh.

With that, Daniels and Anderson quickly and gratefully departed.

"I don't know how you can defend people like that," said Anderson while driving Daniels home. "The kid isn't worth saving. And I'm a doctor saying that!"

"You learn not to take it personal," Daniels said. "Besides, this case isn't about him. It's about justice. I now truly think he's innocent and that the police are railroading him. I simply can't have it. Society can't have that. But society can't stop it. We can. Besides, that was all bravado from Biff. He's a punk, but even punks can be scared shitless."

"Can you trust him on the stand?" Anderson asked.

"I may not call him to testify; not sure yet," Daniels said. "The DA's going to skewer Biff. Our trump card is the DNA evidence. You, my man, are my ticket to serving truth, justice and the American way."

"OK, Superman," laughed Anderson. "Of course, Superman never gets dehydrated."

"My God, you do have a personality after all, Doc!" marveled Daniels.

"Of course. It's just somewhat buried in my DNA."

Chapter 22

Ashley and Daniels, after knocking off a small bottle of Merlot as well as two large glasses of water to keep him hydrated, were in a reflective mood lying in bed after a particularly sensual sexual encounter.

"I think L.A. brings out the romantic in you," Ashley said. "You seem more relaxed here."

"It's strange," Daniels said, "but I do. This murder/rape trial has made it crystal clear to me that I am tired of that entire criminal defense scene. I want to win that trial and focus on this fully. Even if Coffeemate has a short run, this is a dream come true. And I will savor every precious moment."

"I'm somewhat surprised at your admission," she said, "but obviously thrilled to hear it. Jack Daniels is the man I fell in love with, not John Daniels. I'm not comfortable in your legal world, which subconsciously is why I likely was such a bitch at times in the context of that world."

"For many years John Daniels was my life, and John squelched Jack Daniels from surfacing for years. I don't regret a moment of my legal career. I was and am proud of being an elite criminal defense attorney. But singing always intrigued me and all the years I sang in the shower I knew I had talent. Sometimes I would sing in the shower so long that my skin would dry out and get itchy, especially in the winter. And then I would feel like a pussy for having to use a skin moisturizer."

"You are a pussy," she teased. "What next? A Brazilian wax to match mine?"

He rolled over and kissed her gently.

"All this is a dream come true," Daniels said. "Performing live. The upcoming recording sessions. The CD. The tour. But most of all, my music world led me to you. You were and are the most tangible piece of evidence, if you will excuse the legal term, of my rebirth as Jack Daniels. I had given up any serious consideration of having another serious relationship after my wife passed. And then there was you, so different and so utterly intriguing and intoxicating and incandescent in every way. I love you unconditionally and you have shown the same to me. Your life force simply lights the blue flame on my soul's pilot light."

Ashley couldn't control the tears of joy gently rolling over her high, chiseled cheek bones.

"Daniels, I have never met anyone like you. At first I thought we might be an unlikely pair, a strangle coupling. But the instant connection was undeniable and the chemistry, despite some significant challenges, has grown ever more incredible. I will love you intensely forever and a day."

"What happens on the second day after forever?" he quipped.

"That will be the twelfth of never," she laughed, playfully slapping his chest. "Now let's get some sleep. You have a recording session tomorrow morning at 8, and need I remind you that would be 5 in the a.m. in Braxton."

"And in two nights we have our first concert in L.A.," Daniels said. "That has me amped. Of course, I will have to work on my trial prep some tomorrow night and during the day Tuesday."

"Drink more water in case the toll of all that work puts you on a caffeine binge and dehydrates you again."

"Maybe I should get rip-roaring drunk like Jim Morrison or the lead singer for The Prairie Dogs."

"Don't knock The Prairie Dogs vocalist," Ashley said. "If it weren't for his DUI, the recording studio wouldn't have been available to us so soon."

"I'll drink to that," Daniels laughed and then downed another shot of water.

The next morning Coffeemate had an exquisite recording session. The guys were totally in that zone where everything was in sync and they never sounded more dynamic, more powerful, more pulsating, and when need be, more melodic.

Daniels' voice was pitch perfect, and everybody in the studio swore it was Jim Morrison come back to life.

Cy Schwartzman attended the session and at one point muttered aloud to himself: "Damn, this guy sounds better than Morrison!"

All the guys were superbly energized by the opportunity and they all played with a virtuosity that transcended their previous best -- individually and collectively -- on The Doors' covers and their new original material.

Toad on lead guitar, Ziggy on rhythm guitar and Bones on bass plucked those strings with all the skill that Stradivarius had once worked maple.

Pudge's massive arms delivered the most denture-loosening and ear-shattering percussion since John Henry was a steel-driving man.

But above it all there was The Voice of Daniels/Morrison.

After the three-hour session, Coffeemate was bathed in sweat and awash in the realization that their CD was going to be a killer.

"Your fresh material was amazing," Schwartzman gushed to Toad and Daniels.

"Don't credit me," Daniels said. "Toad and Ziggy wrote the bulk of the new tracks, with Bones and Pudge pitching in as well. I was the only one who didn't contribute."

"We tried to capture how The Doors' music would evolve three, four decades later," Toad said.

"You did," Schwartzman gushed. "Absolutely. I'm not sure which new track we should feature for radio play, either *Summer Killing* or *Lost In Hell*. I just know we won't get any air play on Christian radio with those two."

"If we did, that would insult the memory of Morrison," bellowed Pudge.

"I couldn't be more pleased," Schwartzman said. "For Day One in the studio, this was awesome. You laid down a great base of material we can work with and you obviously will have several more sessions here. But for now, rest that voice, Daniels. Tomorrow night at the ritzy Mystic Club in Glendale the folks here in L.A. are gonna hear how fabulous you are performing live."

The Coffeemate gang celebrated the day's great studio session with a delicious dinner at a swank Beverly Hills restaurant, courtesy of Daniels and Ashley.

"It's a wonder that Toad, Ziggy, Bones and Pudge can eat with their tongues hanging out over all the Hollywood babes stuffed like sardines in their skimpy dresses," Ashley giggled softly to Daniels over their lobster and filet. "And if your tongue starts hanging out too, my dear, I just may have to snip something that hangs below your belt."

Daniels' chuckles were halted in midstream by a text from Douglas Fairbanks, who wasn't inquiring how the recording session went.

Fairbanks' text read simply: "Crisis. Biff beaten up in prison. Albert Swanson pressured the judge to have his trial moved up on the court docket and have it start next week. Apparently the DA is all for it, thinking you're distracted in L.A. and not ready to go to trial. The mayor says Biff is not safe in Miller County Prison because the warden and Fred Driscoll are golfing buddies."

Suddenly Daniels wanted to make an umbrella stand out of Al Swanson's feet.

Ashley saw the ghoulish scowl on Daniels' face as he furiously texted Fairbanks bank with: "Old Man Swanson is a stupid fuck. You should have tried to talk him out of it. I will call you and Doc Anderson in the morning. Find out all you can about the attack on Biff. Perhaps this will play into our hands about police conspiracy. Not sure. How bad is Biff?"

Fairbanks texted back: "Black eye, lost a front tooth, couple broken ribs. He can stand trial."

Daniels' return text: "Make sure his tooth still is out when we go to trial. Hope that damn black eye heals slowly. We may have to give him another black eye the day before the trial."

Daniels quickly kissed Ashley on the cheek and said aloud to the table: "Enjoy your meal and the drinks, boys. But don't get drunk. Tomorrow night's gig is important to us. Ashley and I are heading home. I have to do some trial work."

"Home to Braxton? What about the concert?" Toad asked angrily.

"Not Braxton, our L.A. home!" Daniels said. "This is our home. Don't disturb us when you get back to our L.A. home tonight. I will see you guys at the sound check tomorrow."

On the drive from the restaurant to their rented L.A. home, all Daniels said was: "Al Swanson just screwed his own son up the ass. Biff got his pretty looks messed up a bit in jail. Swanson panicked and pressured the judge to begin the trial next week."

"Next fucking week!" screeched an incredulous Ashley. "Oh, fuck! We have another concert next week plus more recording sessions. What are we gonna do?"

"We'll figure it the hell out," Daniels said, his voice trailing off as he got lost in his thoughts.

One thing about Daniels, he had an inordinate ability to relax and concentrate in the midst of pressure. That ice water in his veins was as important to him as his legal experience and savvy.

But for the moment, he was somewhat reeling from the latest example of why having talent in two distinct dimensions can be a tyranny.

Chapter 23

Cy Schwartzman, Albert Swanson, Toad, Ziggy, Bones, Pudge and Ashley all had one thing in common: They wanted to kill Daniels.

After a whirlwind week in which Daniels and Coffeemate were brilliant performing at the Mystic Club in Glendale and laying down some tracks in the studio while Daniels and Ashley also squeezed in two cross-country trips to Braxton for trial prep, the new week dawned with Daniels set to really get busy.

"Busier than a guy servicing a whole harem of chorus girls," an upbeat Daniels said over an early breakfast Monday morning with Ashley.

"And loving every damn minute of it," scolded Ashley. "You get off on all this shit. An adrenaline junkie to the first degree."

"Have no other choice," Daniels said. "I'm stoked."

Daniels knew that you had to fight the dragon, or in his case, dragons any way you could.

After two days of jury selection in Braxton in which Daniels populated the jury with a bright gene pool who could understand and appreciate the complexities and nuances of DNA evidence, Daniels was flying to L.A. Tuesday night for a Wednesday studio session and concert in Santa Barbara.

The impending trip didn't please Al Swanson.

"If my son fries, you fry too you bastard!" he screamed at Daniels after Tuesday's jury selection had wrapped up.

"Relax, Prince Albert or I will put you back in your can," Daniels quipped. "The jury selection went fine. Doug Fairbanks will be here to tie up loose ends Wednesday and I will take the redeye Wednesday night from LAX and be here in time for Thursday's opening statements to the jury. Just say I had to schmooze Judge Levy to grant a one-day postponement in the start of the trial. Turns out that the judge was a helluva Doors fan growing up."

"You are something else," said Fairbanks, who also was there along with Doc Anderson. "But no problem. Bite my tongue, but I totally believe now that you're a brilliant attorney."

"Thank you very much," grinned Daniels. "That means a lot coming from a swashbuckler such as yourself."

"If your flight is delayed, I'll have you arrested," Swanson snapped, definitely not sharing Daniels' and Fairbanks' Kumbaya outlooks.

"With one of Driscoll's cops?" asked Daniels with a laugh.

"You're joking at a serious time like this?" asked Swanson, his pupils and nostrils the size of silver dollars.

"Got my game face swagger on, Al," said Daniels. His suddenly stern face punctuated that he was dead serious and that matters were as sticky as pine tar.

With that, Daniels abruptly left. He power walked to the parking garage, sprinted up the stairs to the third level, jumped in his car and embarked for the Philly airport. Along the way he worked on his opening statement to the jury. He never memorized his opening statements. Unlike his socks drawer, his mind was amazingly organized. Daniels had a remarkable ability to simply and concisely expand upon talking points. He never forgot to mention pertinent points. By the time he delivered his opening statement he simply knew it from hands-on experience. Sort of like Ashley's curvy backside.

Deep in legal thought, the minutes and miles were passing as quickly as Daniels was passing tractor trailers and pokey drivers who undoubtedly were either tortoises or snails in a previous life.

Until the notorious Blue Route that links the infamous Surekill Expressway with I-95 to the airport suddenly became more clogged than the shower drain in a harem's shower.

"Fuck me!" bellowed Daniels, who suddenly was more fucked than a $25-dollar-a-trick whore in a silver mining camp.

Daniels switched from his favorite rock station and punched the dial for KYW-Radio, all news all the time that gives traffic on the twos.

Four minutes later a steaming Daniels got the bad news from KYW: A tractor-trailer had decided to jackknife on a perfectly clear evening and spill crates of live chickens across three lanes of the Blue Route.

Suddenly Bobby Vinton's *Blue Velvet* started playing in Daniels' mind.

Then gallows humor took over.

"If chickens are yellow, this now is the damn Yellow Route!" Daniels said to his steering wheel, which didn't even break a grin.

Sitting in gridlocked traffic of Tolstoy length, Daniels knew he was facing a road fraught with peril and likely was going to miss his 9:30 p.m. flight to LAX since it already was 7:10 p.m. He knew that unless many of the stalled motorists ahead had portable grills in their vehicles and roasted all those chickens ASAP, he was going to have to get a room near the Philly airport and hopefully catch the first flight out in the morning and hope that he didn't miss too much of the recording session.

He figured he would spend the down time stalled in his sleek Mercedes Benz consulting his trial notes and prepping his opening statement. But first he figured he had better alert Ashley.

"Got a helicopter handy that he can pick me up from the roof of my Benz here on the Blue Route?" he asked, trying to keep the mood light -- at least to her. "Apparently a tractor-

143

trailer has jackknifed up ahead and there are crates with live chickens in them all over three lanes. Just call me fucking lucky."

"Hello, Mr. Fucking Lucky," Ashley said, also trying not to have Daniels' mood explode like a Fourth of July firecracker.

"I'm going to miss my flight I would assume," Daniels said. "You had better call the guys in L.A. and tell them I may have to join their recording session in progress unless Cy Schwartzman wants to send a private jet to come get me tonight at the Philly airport."

"Do you think he would?" Ashley asked.

"Did Jim Morrison have self-control?" asked Daniels, getting irritated. "Of course not."

"He might if you paid for the private jet," Ashley said. "Seriously."

"You know, you just might have something," Daniels said. "I have Cy's number in my phone and I'm gonna call him now."

"Let me know what he says," Ashley said. "Good luck. Stay calm. Bye."

Daniels exhaled deeply, called Cy and when the super agent answered, he heard Daniels/ parody of Morrison singing in his ear:

Find me an exit
My not so beautiful friend
Find me an exit
My not so beautiful friend
There's congestion all over the road
Can't travel the highway, baby
Not making me a happy camper
Need to fly west, baby

"What the hell you doing, Daniels?" snapped Schwartzman.

"I need a small favor," Daniels said, "if you want me at tomorrow's recording session on time."

"Send a cab over to your L.A. home because your car broke down?" asked Schwartzman with obvious sarcasm and annoyance.

"Send me a private jet to pick me up at the Philly airport tonight and fly me back to L.A. overnight," Daniels said softly.

"What! Are you out of your mind? What are the odds I can find a private jet so quickly? And who the hell is gonna pay for it? Not me, buddy. You! Why can't you fly commercial?"

"I'm stuck in a damn traffic jam on the way to the airport from Braxton, where we finished jury selection today."

"I told you that this fucking trial would fuck things up," Schwartzman said. "Let me make a couple phone calls and get back to you. If I didn't think you will become a big money-maker for me, I'd tell you to make a U-turn and go back to being a lawyer full time.

"Can't make a U-turn with miles of traffic up my ass," Daniels said. "I'll pay for the plane. Just find me one. And make sure it's safe. Enough rockers have died in airplane crashes. I don't want to be another Otis Redding or Ricky Nelson or John Denver or Jim Croce or Stevie Ray Vaughan or Ronnie VanZant or Buddy Holly or Richie Valens."

"Relax," Schwartzman said. "You're supposed to be Jim Morrison. He either died from heart failure in his Paris flat bathtub or a Paris nightclub toilet stall from a heroin overdose. Either way, stay the hell away from Paris and heroin. I'll call you back as soon as I can."

His car still stuck to the same spot on the Blue Route like a glob of cereal clotted to the side of the bowl, Daniels reviewed his opening statement to the jury. He knew it was vital to make it clear that while Biff was clearly no choir boy and was an entitled brat; he was not a killer/rapist because he was too much of a selfish party boy to risk being executed or sentenced to life in prison.

But Daniels felt his primary theme in his opening statement was to establish from the get-go that the jury should not trust the message that the prosecution was going to present them. His message had to be that they couldn't trust the messenger because the messenger would be lying to them. That if police officers were lying to them; if they weren't testifying truthfully, there was no reason for them to believe that all of the physical evidence the prosecution collected and presented was as reliable as it suggested. Furthermore, there was a compelling reason for them to suspect incompetence and corruption of the physical evidence.

While lost in his legal concentration, he was startled when his smartphone rang. It was Schwartzman.

"OK, I've arranged a private jet charter for you, rich boy," Schwartzman said. "Usually they require a minimum of 24 hours' notice but I schmoozed them with eight tickets to a Springsteen concert next month. So they will take off at 2 a.m. tomorrow your time and land at LAX at 4 a.m. tomorrow my time. By the way, it's $1,800 an hour. A nice little piece of change I would say."

"Damn, almost 10 grand," Daniels said sadly. "Do you think I can write that off as a business expense?"

"If you got a shark accountant like I do," Schwartzman said, punctuated by an evil laugh.

By the time traffic got moving again an eternity or two later, Daniels had composed his opening statement to the jury and was comfortable with it. On the remaining portion of the drive to the airport, he called Ashley to tell her about the cost of the private jet service.

"Shit, 10 grand would buy me a ton of awesome jewelry," she said. "Promise me this is your last trial or I'm going to skin you like a grape."

"Man, you don't have to beg me on that," Daniels said. "I'm getting too old to balance all this. The adrenaline rush is wearing off."

"And the insanity rush is taking over," Ashley said, laughing. "Please be careful. Hopefully that private jet isn't an old crate with wings. And hopefully the pilot isn't drunk."

Several hours later Daniels was sitting in the private jet, which hardly was a flying crate. It was called a Heavy Jet and was designed for cross-country flights. It could seat 12 so he had plenty of leg room and his choice of seating options.

The pilot also was a comfort. Captain Spence Maxwell said he was a former combat pilot in Iraq and Afghanistan and an Air Force Academy grad. He also was a Doors' fan but his voice hardly resembled Morrison's or Daniels' as he sang an off-key version of *Light My Fire*.

Captain Maxwell was singing a different song two hours later when a bad storm had the Heavy Jet just about doing barrel rolls.

He started singing a playful rewrite of the Doors' *The End* on the intercom from the cockpit to the passenger area:

This damn well could be it
So I need a friend
We could just go splat
And that would be a messy end

"Knock off the jokes, Captain!" Daniels replied, only half-kidding.

"Got ya!" laughed Maxwell. "This is a rough mother. But nothing this jockey can't handle. If I get you to LAX alive, can I score a couple tickets to your concert tomorrow night?"

"Hell, you get a dozen tickets and the chance to sit in on a set if we get there alive," laughed Daniels, who didn't feel much like laughing.

"Well, you're on partner," said the captain. "Enough chit-chat or you're gonna get an Iowa barn silo up your ass!"

Captain Maxwell was up to the herculean task and finally the Heavy Jet was out of danger. Not a moment too soon because Daniels was dying to sprint to the toilet to wash the vomit that had splashed on his shirt. It was the first time in his life he had gotten sick from motion sickness and he couldn't find the damn vomit bag in time. Fortunately, there was more than one place to sit in the cabin because there was a nice puddle of puke on the floor where he was sitting.

When they finally landed at LAX, a scent of vomit still trailed Daniels even though he had changed shirts. Captain Maxwell didn't seem to mind the odor. A $1,000 gratuity will do wonders for a guy's mood.

"Don't forget my tickets to your concert tomorrow night," the captain reminded.

"They will be at Will Call," Daniels said, his last word cut short by a violent sneeze.

"That sounded nasty," Maxwell said.

Before Daniels could respond, there was a sequel sneeze with even more percussion.

"Damn, I don't want to get a freaking cold," Daniels said. "We're in the recording studio tomorrow plus we have the evening concert."

"Tell the band to play louder to drown out your voice somewhat," offered the captain. "I'm sure The Doors did that some nights when Morrison was drunk or high or both on stage."

"I'll drink Scotch whiskey all night long," laughed Daniels, who was beginning to sound nasally.

"That line was in *Deacon Blues* by Steely Dan," said Captain Maxwell.

"Right on, Sky Pilot," countered Daniels.

"That would be The Animals," laughed Maxwell.

"Correcto mundo," said Daniels. "See you at the gig tomorrow night in Santa Barbara."

Daniels woke up the next morning with a full-blown cold and a sore throat. He wasn't a guy who got sick often, so he would be irritated as hell when he did.

"I don't have time for this fucking shit," he said to his face in the bathroom vanity mirror.

Of course, the recording session in the studio was your basic cluster fuck. Daniels, his throat getting rawer with every note, sounded like a Jim Morrison who had gargled razor blades along with his Southern Comfort.

Cy Schwartzman, more pissed than a 95-year-old who misplaced his Depends, cut the session short.

"You wasted a lot of money on that jet charter last night, Daniels," he said. "For what? We can't lay down any of these tracks. You sounded like shit. You got the cold because you're worn down from burning the candle at both ends."

"Everybody gets colds," Daniels, in no mood for a scolding, fired back. "Besides, we're just trying to enhance tracks we already did and which already sound great."

"What happened to Daniels the perfectionist?" asked a belligerent Toad. "You know how important this is to us. Cy is right."

"Win that goddamn trial twinkle quick and focus on the music," commanded Pudge.

"Amen, brother!" echoed Bones.

Even Ziggy the Pipsqueak piled on.

"A lack of sleep will make anybody sick," he said. "You sound like shit. We had better play loudly tonight in Santa Barbara to drown you out."

"We'll pull a Milli Vanilli lip syncing and just play our covers tonight while we play an old Doors album on the sound system," said Daniels, his words coated with sarcasm.

"Instead, get a Z-Pak from your doctor and drink a lot of honey and tea this afternoon," Schwartzman said.

Which is exactly what Daniels did -- with a big assist from his doctor in Braxton whose office phoned in a prescription to a drug store near Daniels' rented L.A. home.

Daniels didn't speak the rest of the day, saving his voice for the concert. He even refused to talk to Ashley, restricting their communication to text messages. She, of course, sided with the band and Cy. Daniels felt like an Army of One and the other side had a hundred thousand warriors. With those odds, he was in for a rough fight.

They all underestimated Daniels. He had an enormous capacity to rise to the occasion and close the show, like Ali used to do in the closing seconds of a round. Granted, he didn't quite sound like himself that night in Santa Barbara. But the passion and the fury with which he attacked each song was astonishing and the capacity crowd -- including Captain Maxwell, his wife and friends -- absolutely loved him.

"Hot damn," Toad chirped after they closed with *Light My Fire*. "You sure pulled that one out of your ass."

"You sounded raw and sexy," cracked Pudge, "and I say that confident in my masculinity."

"You are a warrior," said Cy. "Now go home and close the show with that damn trial!"

Toad and Bones then quickly drove Daniels to LAX to catch the red-eye back to Philly. Daniels rarely slept on a plane, even on red-eyes, but this time he slept like a drugged zombie. The flight attendant had to awaken him when they were about to land in Philly. Still bleary-eyed with terminal exhaustion and his cold giving his Z-Pak the finger, Daniels was lucky to stay awake and fortunate enough not to encounter any major traffic jams on his drive back to Braxton.

He got to the courthouse 30 minutes before the trial was scheduled to begin. Never has a criminal defense attorney in the most important trial of his life faced making an opening statement to the jury feeling like the total piece of sick shit that John Daniels felt like that morning.

When Biff sat down at the defendant's table and saw the washed-out Daniels, he politely and politically said, "Holy fuck, are you freaking hung over, dude?"

Biff's words snapped like a cold towel in Daniels' face. Another adrenaline rush charged through his arteries. It was time to play some legal rock and roll.

Chapter 24

Judge Marv Levy, a ponderous man and former heavyweight boxer, once had been called "one thick fuck" by a frustrated attorney in the courtroom.

The remark was only appropriate physically. Mentally, Judge Levy was lean and mean.

Judge Levy's gavel got an early workout when Daniels' opening statement to the jury clearly signaled that his defense was to put the entire Braxton police department and former chief Fred Driscoll on trial. If was almost as if Biff Swanson was merely a victim who wasn't even on trial.

The uproar in the packed courtroom was raucous and bellowing the loudest was Big Jim Gallagher, the DA.

"You can't object to an opening statement," Judge Levy scolded Gallagher three times. "You know better."

After his opening statement the judge ordered a sidebar conference with Daniels and Gallagher.

"Where the hell are you going with this, Daniels?" asked Levy, his pupils big enough to dance on.

"Yeah, where the hell are you going with this?" echoed Gallagher. "You have no case so you are going to put on a circus and make a mockery out of the judicial system. You know this trial is getting national media attention and you are turning it into a cheap publicity stunt to market your ridiculous singing career. You have been an esteemed litigator. Don't go out a disgrace."

"Refrain from the hysterics and theatrics," Judge Levy admonished the DA. "This is my courtroom."

Levy then stared two holes into Daniels' skull.

"Be very careful, John," he warned. "Watch your P's and Q's."

"And not my F's and U's?" asked Daniels mischievously. By the grin on his face, you would have never have known that he felt sicker than a guy whose wife had just walked in on him getting a blow job. In fact, Daniels felt so physically weak that Ashley, looking as prim and proper as she possibly could two rows behind the defense team table, was praying that he wouldn't faint.

"You want get to get hit with contempt of court on the first day?" asked Levy.

Daniels' opening remarks to the jury had sent a chill of concern up and down Gallagher's spine while at the same time sending a chill of dread up and down Fred Driscoll's spine, a chill of hope up and down Al Swanson's spine, and a chill of amazement up and down Douglas Fairbanks' spine.

Daniels' motivation was cunning and simple. He needed to establish territorial imperative. The first couple weeks of a trial usually the prosecution is ahead because it's the prosecution's case -- the defense hasn't put on a case yet. From the get-go Daniels wanted to put the defense team out in front. He wanted to put the prosecution on its heels from day one of the trial, to control the case. He would challenge every single piece of evidence the prosecution entered. He and Doc Anderson knew that the prosecution was going to present a case with a lot of holes and they were confident that they had found each one. And that the jury would respond to that.

Daniels' mission was to turn the Biff Swanson murder/rape trial into a trial of the Braxton police department, most specifically Fred Driscoll even if Al Swanson had fired him. Daniels totally planned to exploit and capitalize on the feud between Driscoll and Al Swanson and paint the black picture that not only had the Braxton police sloppily mishandled key DNA evidence but under the direct and indirect influence of their then police chief had willingly and deliberately planted and compromised evidence to frame Biff Swanson.

Daniels had gotten right to the point with all the sledgehammer force of George Foreman in his prime hitting the heavy bag.

Daniels knew that complex DNA testimony could be harder for a jury to decipher than a trig textbook. Some juries were like a wet Post-it note: Nothing seemed to stick. The last thing Daniels wanted was a jury to be sequestered in confusion. He was walking a tightrope that was slicker than a glacier. While the trial pivoted on DNA evidence, he wanted to keep the focus lasered on the credibility, or lack thereof, of the police and prosecution.

"Ladies and gentlemen, I have nothing but the highest respect for the law and the police," Daniels began. "I have spent my life in the pursuit of justice. However, the law is not always on your side. The human element for whatever reason can contaminate the law. Which is why we have courtrooms and trials to balance the scales of justice.

"We will prove to you beyond a reasonable shadow of a doubt that the Braxton police have framed Biff Swanson because of a heated feud between his father, the mayor of Braxton, and the police chief of Braxton, now fired by the mayor. The cops couldn't find the rapist/killer of 17-year-old Melanie Driscoll, the daughter of Fred Driscoll, so in their rage, grief and frustration they decided to make a sacrificial lamb out of Biff Swanson.

"Simply put, we will prove to you that you cannot trust the prosecution because the police, the messenger, will be lying to you. Which means that you really can't trust the message they will be presenting to you. So if you have police officers that will be lying to you, that won't be testifying to you truthfully, there's no reason for you to believe that all of the physical evidence that they've collected and will present is as reliable as they will suggest. There's reason for you to fear incompetence and worse: corruption of the physical evidence. And you certainly can't trust the story they're telling about Biff Swanson. This is a case where the cops are closing ranks. Even the DA here is a former state cop."

That, of course, had Big Jim Gallagher leaping out of his seat like a Jack In The Box on crank.

After Gallagher had screamed "Objection" loud enough to break the sound barrier, Daniels -- after a pregnant silence that seemed to last for an eternity and a day -- continued his opening statement.

"You cannot trust their DNA test results because they had corrupt and incompetent people collecting the evidence and preserving the evidence," he said. "That evidence is only as good as the people who collect it. We will shatter the integrity of their evidence collection process. And shatter the myth that Biff Swanson, while a despicable young man in many ways, is a rapist and a murderer. He is neither."

Daniels had the distinct advantage of going second because the prosecution's opening statement is first. Gallagher had gone into great detail outlining the evidence, most of it DNA-related, against Biff Swanson.

From the get-go, Daniels aggressive attack on the credibility of the DNA results compromised Big Jim Gallagher's genetic blueprint to link Biff to the rape/homicide.

Daniels knew that evidence collection at crime scenes, especially when done by rank-and-file police officers, sometimes was flawed. There were times they were dealing with miniscule amounts of blood or semen or hair or bodily fluids or saliva or a piece of clothing that the samples were either consciously or unconsciously or sloppily handled before being sent to the state police crime lab in Bethlehem.

The DNA evidence was critical to the prosecution's case because it could not find Biff Swanson's fingerprints at the crime scene.

Two crucial points that Daniels masterfully used to helpfully cast doubt in the jury were the DNA samples the police already had from a previous Biff arrest and the unusual speed of the report being sent back from the state police laboratory in Greensburg.

Addressing the first point, Daniels told the jury in his opening statement:

"The defendant was previously arrested by the Braxton police for hitting a guy and breaking a window at The Juicy Oyster. They already had samples of his DNA. They planted that DNA at the rape/murder scene because some of Biff's blood there had EDTA on it, a chemical that's an anticoagulant that's not found in the human body; it's only found in test tubes. So we will prove beyond the shadow of a doubt that the police planted blood collected from Biff's incident at The Juicy Oyster from the test tubes onto the deceased's blouse. Moreover, the splatter pattern on the blouse was such that it was consistent only with blood having been poured on the blouse, and not with blood having hit the front of the blouse and then soaking through it. The prosecution claims that a paper towel with Biff Swanson's DNA was found at the crime scene, suggesting Biff used it to wipe his penis after the rape. Easy to plant, we contend. And if a guy like Biff just raped and choked a girl to death, do you think he would worry about a little semen on his penis? And if so, stupid enough to wipe it with a paper towel and leave it just lying there on the girl's stomach?"

The jury absolutely was transfixed hearing all that. And all the jurors had to do was look at the faces of Fred Driscoll and Jim Gallagher to know that Daniels' had hit a jagged nerve in the prosecution.

What Daniels was doing in his opening statement was not just giving an overview of his case, he actually was presenting the case and then waiting to validate it with Doc Anderson's expert witness testimony and by making Fred Driscoll more uncomfortable on the stand than a guy having a root canal without Novocain. The danger in Daniels' approach was that he was laying all his cards on the table very early, giving the prosecution a major head's up and ample time to refute his assertions. Daniels, however, was confident that his opening statement would be so utterly powerful that it would remain indelible throughout the trial. And he was equally as confident that the prosecution simply couldn't disprove his allegations because they were in fact true.

Addressing the second point of how remarkably quick the Braxton police had received a report on the DNA sample collection from the rape/murder, Daniels said:

"It is our contention that the Braxton police and the DA, a former state cop, had the findings of the DNA sample evidence collected at the crime scene unbelievably fast-tracked to Braxton. A rush to judgment? A rush to frame poor Biff?"

That, of course, caused such a ruckus in the courtroom that it resembled a heavy metal concert. And it had Big Jim Gallagher going off like a geyser *and* an erupting volcano.

After the uproar finally subsided, Daniels, his voice suddenly switching from the dramatic to a matter-of-fact tonality, calmly continued:

"With more local departments than ever submitting DNA material, there's a huge backlog," he said. "It's not uncommon to see a year-and-a-half backlog when dealing with property crimes. There is a faster response when it involves violent crimes against people. But two weeks, the time it took for Braxton to get the results back from the state police lab, has to be an Olympic and world record, ladies and gentlemen."

The media went viral over Daniels' opening statement to the jury. Social media, conventional media, tabloid media, they were all over it. It was sensational publicity for Daniels and Schwartzman. Criminal defense attorneys who weighed in on CNN, Fox News and MSNBC were all over the lot on Daniels' bold gambit -- saying he had tipped off the prosecution who now could adjust, that he was insane; and that he, along with Doc Anderson, simply and brilliantly were following in the footsteps of Johnnie Cochran and Barry Schneck in the O.J. Simpson trial.

As it turned out, the prosecution couldn't adjust much. The cops were dirty; they had planted and altered DNA evidence, and had no choice but lie about it unless they were willing to confess. They didn't have to confess. Daniels was a master in the courtroom, outclassing the prosecution and finding each and every hole in their case. The jury ate it up, as it did the riveting testimony of Doc Anderson. Daniels left a string of numb and mumbling and stumbling cops from the stand.

Speaking of the stand, the two marquee folks perched there were Biff Swanson and Fred Driscoll. Daniels played both like Michael Jordan played hoops. Rather well, for you non-basketball fans. Daniels had decided that Biff being Biff actually would pay off on the stand because he wanted the jury to know that he was a punk and to underscore why the police chief and cops didn't mind framing an asshole like the kid. When Biff was sworn in, Daniels asked Biff to smile, revealing the front tooth that the prison guards had knocked out.

"Nice missing tooth, pal," Daniels said with a wicked smile.

"No shit! Damn prison guards!" Biff snarled.

The judge and the DA uttered shouts of "Watch your language, son!" and "Objection!" respectively, with the perfect tandem of synchronized swimmers.

"Biff lost a tooth, got a black eye that you still can see somewhat, and suffered a couple broken ribs that still ache when his daddy hugs him," Daniels said calmly. "Apparently his prison guards were a little gung-ho in providing Biff with a martial arts lesson to protect him from the other inmates. I'm sure those fellows meant no harm."

Daniels' casual demeanor blunted the DA's objection while simultaneously sticking like Super Glue to the jurors' impressionable minds.

Daniels then caught the kid, his old man, and the entire courtroom rather off-guard by asking Biff, "You're a selfish, spoiled punk, aren't you?"

Biff, of course, denied it.

"Man, not me," Biff said. "Whose side are you on, anyway? Aren't you supposed to be my defense attorney?

"I'm on the side of justice and truth," Daniels replied. "Tell me, you also are quite the ladies man, aren't you?"

Biff, as superficial as ever, smiled like somebody had just put a candle in his mouth.

"Put it this way, I never have to beg for it, if you know what I mean," said Biff, winking.

Daniels was so happy hearing that response he wanted to kiss Biff on the lips.

"A guy like you never would have to force himself on a woman, now would you?" he asked.

"Hell, uh, I mean heck no," Biff said.

"You would never have to rape a woman, would you?" Daniels asked.

"Me? Of course not. Man, I didn't rape Melanie. Why would I have to? She loved it when we had sex. Why would I rape and kill a girl I could have with the snap of my finger?"

Daniels looked at the jury and solemnly said, "Now I know why guppies eat their young."

The jury and spectators, shocked and surprised, responded with spontaneous laughter.

Needless to say, Daniels, the master of manipulation, had a piranha's appetite for the kill.

"No more questions, your honor," Daniels quickly added as a jackknifing exclamation point.

He then looked at Fred Driscoll. If eyes could kill, Daniels would be deader than Jim Morrison.

Big Jim Gallagher looked like he literally wanted to grill Biff on the stand and eat him after coating him in tartar sauce.

"Son," Gallagher said in a sarcastic tone, "rape and murder are the two worst crimes a human being can commit. Despicable. Which is why you are facing the death penalty. Which is why we are all here so our esteemed jury can decide if you did indeed in a cold-blooded premeditated manner rape and murder 17-year-old Melanie Driscoll. While there were no eyewitnesses, the evidence has your name written all over the rape and murder despite your desperate defense team's wild allegations discrediting the physical, scientific evidence as well as our honorable city police force.

"When a criminal defense attorney attacks the credibility of Braxton's finest in the rape/murder trial involving the then police chief's daughter, I can't begin to tell you how much that makes my bile boil as well as the bile in all good citizens of our community."

"Objection!" screamed Daniels. "There is no way the DA would be able to take the temperature of the bile in all good citizens of our community."

That, of course, triggered a few giggles in the courtroom as well as the jury box.

"Overruled," the judge quickly said while pounding his gavel to beat back the laughter.

"Not to turn this place into a circus," continued Gallagher, "so I will cut to the chase: Did you rape and murder Melanie Driscoll?

Biff looked more bored than ever hearing that question.

He yawned and then replied: "Like I told Daniels, why would I rape somebody I could do whenever I wanted to? And I hate blood and violence. The only time I ever hit a guy was in that bar fight, and now you guys are using my DNA from that arrest to frame me for a crime I didn't commit. I wasn't with Melanie that night. Fred Driscoll hated me because he hates my old man because my dad thinks Driscoll is a dirty cop. Simple as that. So Driscoll decided to screw me and my old man by charging me with rape and a murder because he's too dumb a cop to find the real killer. No wonder my old man fired his ass. This trial is fucking bullshit!"

That bugged out the eyeballs of Gallagher and Judge Levy and triggered a surreal combination of a hush and an outburst in the courtroom.

"One more outburst like that, young man, and I will hold you and your attorney in contempt of court," the judge scolded. "Mr. Daniels, please advise your client to respect the decorum of the courtroom."

"I will, your honor," Daniels responded, sounding like a sincere altar boy.

Then Gallagher resumed, adopting the solemn tones of an archbishop at a Good Friday service: "Ladies and gentlemen of the jury, you and you alone are here to judge the fate of this young man. It is a heavy burden to pass judgment in a trial such as this. But I would add in this particular case, the lifting shouldn't be all that heavy. No more questions, your honor."

While walking away from the witness stand, Biff yawned once again and then left a very loud fart. The jury and much of the courtroom laughed out loud.

When Biff returned to the defense table, Daniels whispered in his ear: "You're an asshole, but your testimony when the DA cross-examined you was perfect. And when we adjourn for the day, you had better wipe your ass."

When Fred Driscoll was on the stand, the contempt he had for Daniels seemed to ooze out of his every pore and orifice, especially his mouth. His tone was sharper than a plastic surgeon's scalpel.

Daniels began softly.

"First of all, sir, our condolences on the passing of your daughter," he said in hushed tones.

"Cut the crap, Daniels. She didn't pass. She was raped and murdered by the candy-ass punk you're representing."

Which drew an immediate rebuke from Judge Levy.

"Do not forget this is a courtroom, sir," said the judge.

"I was the police chief of Braxton, your honor, and I certainly know this is a courtroom," said Driscoll, "and ..."

Before Driscoll could finish his sentence, Daniels smoothly interrupted: "And you are a grieving father, and no offense taken. The defense so wants the rapist and killer in this case brought to justice. However, sir, you and I both know that the evidence you have used to arrest and charge my client is not credible and with that evidence compromised and tampered with, you have no evidence to support the charges against Biff Swanson."

"That kid is on trial here, not my former police department," snarled Driscoll.

"You are here to answer questions, not to randomly interject your opinions," scolded the judge.

"It is so understandable that a father who lost a daughter in such a heinous crime would be overwhelmed with grief, anger, heartache and a Biblical cry for vengeance," Daniels said. "But is it not conceivable and possible that in such a state, that would lead that father, then the police chief, to make clouded judgments?"

"Absolutely not!" screamed Driscoll, beginning to sweat profusely.

"Furthermore, wouldn't it not be conceivable and possible that under such circumstances, that police chief's loyal men and women also would have their judgments seemingly clouded in their haste and rush to judgment?"

"Come on, Daniels, you're trying to play me like a drum."

"I am a singer in my side job, not a drummer," said Daniels, suddenly smiling.

The courtroom erupted in laughter, which caused Big Jim Gallagher and Judy Levy to erupt with anger.

"Sorry, your honor," said Daniels, still smiling. And suddenly that smile dramatically turned upside down with warp speed.

"And would you and your subordinates' judgments conceivably and possibly be further clouded by rumors and worries that the mayor, the father of the defendant, was about to allege that you and some of your subordinates were accepting kickbacks from drug dealers?"

"Don't go there, you bastard!" screamed Driscoll, lunging toward Daniels, who quickly stepped aside as the police chief did a comic pratfall worthy of The Three Stooges onto the courtroom floor.

"I am holding you in contempt of court, Mr. Driscoll!" shouted the judge, smashing his gavel with all the percussion of a drummer in a heavy metal band. "But first climb back into that chair and answer his questions."

Scowling and resembling a whipped dog, Driscoll slowly complied.

"And when the mayor did fire you as chief, could some of your former but still loyal subordinates become even more blinded by their desperation, fear and rage and further contaminate the evidence?"

"That is as bogus as your pathetic attempt to be Jim Morrison," shot back Driscoll, fire erupting in his voice and eyes. "Absurd!"

"Then how else to explain how, with the lack of a credible suspect, your Braxton police not only sloppily mishandled key DNA evidence but under the direct and indirect influence of you had willingly and deliberately planted and compromised evidence to frame Biff Swanson and gain revenge against his father, the mayor?" asked Daniels with all the oratory skill of a Winston Churchill.

The courtroom suddenly drew more quiet and eerie than a mummy's tomb. The only audible sound for what seemed an eternity was the labored, heavy breathing of Fred Driscoll, who was sweating through his suit jacket.

"I can't answer that question because none of it is true," said Driscoll, who was so angry he actually was blubbering and losing control of his tear ducts.

"Not true? None of it?" asked Daniels, with a tone of disbelief and arched eyebrows. "Well, if there was no sinister motivation, if you and your force are not corrupt, then you have to be the biggest inept cops in the history of law enforcement because as taxpayers we all should have been appalled and horrified listening to Doc Anderson detail all the gaping holes in the evidence, all the sloppiness in handling the evidence and all the planting of evidence. The real mountain of evidence here is the undisputable fact that there is real, scientific doubt about the evidence implicating Biff. "

Driscoll was almost quivering, a tough ex-cop and a grieving father who had reached too far for blind justice and now was suffering a meltdown in the courtroom and in front of national media.

Daniels pivoted toward the jury but was careful not to address them and strove to make it clear he was technically still speaking to Driscoll although he was actually talking to the jurors.

"Mr. Former Police Chief, Doc Anderson has given those who sit in judgment of Biff Swanson the intellectual and moral permission to question and doubt, if they must, the evidence the prosecution and the police force you commanded have presented. The power of the people needs to fight back against a police state."

"Objection!" bellowed Gallagher.

"Sustained!" bellowed Judge Levy.

"No more questions, your honor," said Daniels, whose walk back to his chair behind the defense table was almost jaunty.

Driscoll sat slumped in the witness chair for a few moments that seemed an eternity, a shell of the man he was when he first sat down. Daniels had husked him like an ear of corn. Character assassination seldom draws blood but it can kill you.

It took all 12 jurors a mere 2 hours and 37 minutes to coalesce around a verdict of not guilty.

As the verdict was announced, Fred Driscoll wept as anger and sorrow welled up in him like a terrible virus; Albert Swanson high-fived anyone within six feet of him; Big Jim Gallagher contemplated killing Daniels; Biff leaned over to Daniels and shouted in his ear, "You DO know that I didn't rape or kill her, don't you?" and then punctuated that with "Hot fucking damn!" and a belch; Ashley unleashed an aurora borealis of a smile and rushed up to hug Daniels; and the boys in the band -- demonstrating yet again that at times they could have geraniums for craniums -- started singing loudly, "This is the end of this legal bullshit" and Judge Levy suffered chest pains and a torn triceps muscle by pounding his gavel until it splintered.

The local, national, tabloid and social media went virally insane and millions tweeted that John Daniels should be nominated to the Supreme Court.

As for John Daniels, it was the ultimate triumph ... a veteran NFL quarterback climaxing his career by winning the Super Bowl. But unlike the Super Bowl, this epic showdown between the law and his music would never be played again.

As for Jack Daniels, it was time to celebrate and then really rock and roll in the morning.

"I love you with all my heart," Daniels whispered in Ashley's ear. "This part of my life now is put to rest. Now all my energies are focused on you, on us and the music."

"Don't get too fucking sappy," said Ashley, tears of joy mutilating her mascara. "You'll lose your Jim Morrison edge."

She was happier than a beachcomber with a metal detector for silver linings.

Chapter 25

Coffeemate went full bore with a ballistic fury on music immediately after the trial ended.

"You only had two days' rest since the trial," Ashley said to Daniels over dinner at a Thai restaurant in downtown L.A.

"Yes, but the trial energized me and I am totally pumped about finishing the album and starting the tour," he said between spoonfuls of Thai noodle soup.

"Where does that leave me, dear?" asked Ashley.

"By my side. You officially are now my and the band's manager. Let's put you on salary … $100,000 a year to start plus benefits to be determined."

"The benefits are getting to sleep with you?"

"That would be one, my dear," Daniels said with a champagne smile and eyes twinkling with sentiment.

They soon wrapped up the CD and then launched an ambitious tour schedule worthy of a headliner group.

"Thanks to the trial going viral and the quality of your original music meshing with The Doors' cover material, you boys are headliners," Cy Schwartzman told the band and Ashley over dinner in Burbank the night before their tour embarked. "We are going to turn Ziggy, Toad, Bones and Pudge into the sexiest men in America. Make room for the groupies."

"My wet dreams come true," laughed Pudge.

"Excuse me, but I was enjoying my cream sauce on my salmon," said Ashley, suddenly nauseous.

Their tour kicked off at the Bell Centre in Montreal, followed by dates at Scotiabank Place in Ottawa, Consol Energy Center in Pittsburgh, First Niagara Center in Buffalo, Philips Arena in Atlanta, Tampa Bay Times Forum in Tampa, Time Warner Cable Arena in Charlotte, Bridgestone Arena in

Nashville, Quicken Loans Arena in Cleveland, Scottrade Center in St. Louis, KFC Yum! Center in Louisville, United Spirit Arena in Lubbock, Xcel Energy Center in St. Paul, American Airlines Center in Dallas, Sprint Center in Kansas City, Pepsi Center in Denver, MGM Grand Garden Arena in Las Vegas, Jobing.com Arena in Glendale, HP Pavilion in San Jose, Staples Center in Los Angeles, and concluding at the in Braxton.

Coffeemate was a sensation on the tour, sprinkling stardust in their wake and generating electric energy that resonated with audiences and music critics. In an era when selling records no longer was easy as selling space heaters in Nome, Alaska, concert tours were a band's lifeblood.

Toad fell in love with an ex-stripper in Buffalo, who told him she had no choice to give up the profession because "taking your fucking clothes off in a fucking city so fucking cold is no fucking fun."

"I must take you home to meet mother," Toad said, who was wooly serious.

Atlanta was a memorable tour stop for Ziggy, who got laid there – his first time in seven years.

"I didn't even care that she was coyote ugly and flatter than a dead man's pulse," Ziggy said the next morning at a group breakfast. "As a hobby, screwing beats the hell out of lawn darts."

"You must have come more than an elephant," observed Pudge.

"No way since he jerks off about six times a day," countered Bones.

"Do you think the New York Philharmonic guys talk like this?" asked Toad.

"Most assuredly," added Ashley.

Pudge got into a teeth-shattering fight in a Louisville nightclub, laying out six guys so dramatically that the media nicknamed him The Louisville Slugger.

Pudge's mug shot went viral, which certainly helped hype the tour. Daniels got Pudge's preliminary hearing postponed until after the tour.

"Those punks called me a fat shit who couldn't carry Ringo's drumsticks," Pudge explained. "Pudge no fucking like that."

Bones, meanwhile, went berserk on the hotel room service in every town and was seriously thinking about updating his nickname.

"If Pudge now is The Louisville Slugger, maybe I can become Pudge," he reasoned.

"And redo the band bios?" asked Toad. "No way! Stay away from the goddamn mountains of pancakes and hash browns, not to mention the banana splits."

Their album *Beyond The Doors* went platinum (selling 1 million copies) on the No Longer Virgin Records label even before the tour ended.

Schwartzman called them backstage in Denver with that delicious news and the band, sans Daniels and Ashley, celebrated with their own version of a Rocky Mountain high. Daniels and Ashley got high on each other.

In Las Vegas the boys, including Daniels, tried their best to mimic the actors in *The Hangover* although none of them got arrested or inked up or slept on a hotel roof.

In San Jose Daniels delighted the audience by crooning Dionne Warwick's *Do you know the way to San Jose*. Minutes later you could have knocked over Daniels with a swizzle stick when Dionne appeared on stage and joined him in a rousing rendition of *Light My Fire.*

By the time they returned to L.A. for the Staples Center gig, they learned their original material on their album had earned them a Grammy nomination for Best Rock Album.

"We ain't just a fucking cover band now, my boys," crowed Toad as they celebrated with champagne flutes.

During the extensive tour, Daniels, whose well-chronicled trial success had made him a celebrity above and beyond the band, made several appearances on network morning talk shows and prime time cable chat fests weighing in on high-profile murder cases and celebrity brushes with the law.

When a prominent Republican was arrested for exposing himself at a Red Hat Ladies dinner, Daniels amused Bill O'Reilly with this quip: "If those sweet old ladies noticed that the guy's pubes all lean to the far right, the judge should give him a stiffer sentence."

"Jim Morrison exposed himself on stage and do you do likewise when you cover him, Daniels?" O'Reilly asked.

"Only if there are a lot of liberals at the concert," countered Daniels.

Daniels' celebrity and glibness already had paid off when he signed to do the speaker circuit for $50,000-a-pop engagements addressing corporate and non-profit charity fundraising dinners, etc.

As the band was flying home to Braxton to finish the tour at the Franklin Arena, they had received word that the NFL had chosen them to play the high-profile Super Bowl halftime show.

"If the Eagles are in the Super Bowl this year, I'll be too nervous to play," Ziggy said.

"No worries," explained Pudge. "They're in last place in the NFC East."

Through all the whirlwind tumult of the tour and Daniels' burgeoning corporate speaking career, Ashley -- trailing an air of manic energy -- was immersed in managing all of it with an expertise, calm, engagement and enjoyment that astonished her.

"Man, who would have thought I was born to do this," she asked Daniels one night after some wicked sex -- a must-do after every concert so Daniels could let off steam from performing the sexually intense Doors covers and Coffeemate's hormone-charged original tracks.

"But most of all, I love how your job transition has energized you and revitalized you," she said, her eyes misting. "I've never seen you so happy. It utterly delights me to see you realize your dream, to share this magic ride with you, and to be totally, helplessly in love with you."

Daniels, misting up himself, smiled and said simply: "You have no idea how much I need you and love you. None of this success would be as sweet if you were not sharing it with me."

They kissed gently and then Ashley abruptly bolted out of their hotel bed to sit at a nearby desk.

"I have to finalize the contracts for the TV commercial you guys are shooting for Geico. You singing a duet with the Geico gecko is gonna be hilarious. I just hope the guys don't piss themselves laughing while they perform."

"What about me?" Daniels asked. "Singing with a gecko is an absurdity I never imagined while studying for the bar exam."

"Life is full of crooked twists and turns," Ashley said.

"Not for us," Daniels said. "We're going straight to the top!"

"Now those are words that stick to your ribs!" she laughed.

Chapter 26

The only thing Braxton, PA and the Hilton Hawaiian Village Waikiki Beach Resort on the island of Oahu have in common is they both inhabit the planet Earth.

While Braxton essentially is as drab and bland as day-old oatmeal, the exotic and lush Hilton Hawaiian Village with its tropical gardens, waterfalls and exotic wildlife is spectacular enough to quicken the pulse in the corpse of Jim Morrison.

Granted, Morrison's corpse was walking along in the body of Jack Daniels, who strolled Waikiki Beach holding hands with Ashley. Their free hands were each holding a Mai Tai.

Perched on beach chairs were the rest of the Coffeemate clan. All of them also were soaking up Mai Tais as well as the sun, which was roasting their foreheads like a rotisserie chicken.

"Damn, the water here is flatter than your skanky last girlfriend," Pudge said to Ziggy.

"Of course it is," lectured Toad. "Waikiki Beach is manmade and they imported the sand from California and Australia."

"Get the hell out," interjected Bones. "This is freaking Hawaii. Where are all the big waves and big-time surfers?"

"Wait until we get to the North Shore," Toad explained. "Wait to you see those 30-foot waves. You'll be scared to dip your toes in the water."

"How do you know all this, Toad?" asked Pudge.

"Google," Toad said.

Coffeemate as well as some friends and relatives of Daniels and Ashley were on Oahu to attend the destination wedding of our favorite couple.

"I hear a lot of Japanese couples get married in Hawaii," Ashley had remarked when Daniels first proposed a Hawaiian wedding.

"They've got a yen for those beautiful sunsets," Daniels had cracked.

Since Ashley was an only child with a deceased father, her only family member in tow for the wedding was her mother, Wanda, who lived in New Orleans, loved voodoo and was a free-spirited, pipe-smoking bottle redhead with an overactive sex drive, and wound up screwing Ziggy and blowing Bones on the same infamous afternoon while in Hawaii.

"That was one gross double play, Mother," scolded Ashley. "My matron of honor, let alone my mother, should have at least a modicum of honor."

"And you've been shacked up with a rock star all this time?" countered Mother Wanda. "I'm more shocked than an electrician doing wiring while standing in a tub overflowing with water."

With both his parents passed on, Daniels brought along his only sibling, his brother Charlie. While he despised country music and looked more like Mister Rogers than Charlie Daniels of the Charlie Daniels Band, this Charlie Daniels had the "Devil Went Down to Georgia" tattooed on his chest, had relocated to Atlanta years earlier, and was an accountant for Coca-Cola.

While Charlie's chest tattoo made him somewhat of an attraction on the beach and poolside, he really didn't add much more to the festivities other than his perfunctory Best Man duties.

Personality wise, Charlie didn't exactly light up a room. If he went to Grauman's Chinese Theater to put his feet in wet cement, he would leave no impression. He was about as cuddly as Rushmore granite.

"Lighten up and have some fun," Jack said to Charlie one evening while the group was watching a gorgeous sunset kiss the Pacific.

"I am," Charlie responded softly. "I'm gorging myself on chocolate-covered macadamia nuts. They go great with Coke."

"Try putting some rum into your Coke while you're here," Jack said.

"I think that violates company rules," Charlie said. "Coca-Cola has spies everywhere. And if they don't see you, Pepsi's spies will!"

"Is he serious?" asked Ashley.

"Absolutely," said Jack.

One day Daniels hired a van with a driver so the group could head up to the North Shore, where they would spend the night at the famous Turtle Bay resort, which is awash with luxurious villas, beach cottages and ocean views of spectacular waves more powerful than a Pudge Klumpf wet fart.

Ashley's hardly reclusive mother wasn't shy at all about immersing herself in the swirling, surging surf and promptly lost her bikini top. Undaunted, she calmly took her time returning to the safety of the beach, where Bones and Ziggy practically wrestled each other for the privilege of covering Wanda's ample breasts with a beach towel.

Needless to say, the boys in the band partied rather heavily at Turtle Bay, soaking in the prodigious ambience and atmosphere along with prodigious amounts of tropical drink concoctions.

They should have shown a tad more restraint because some of them, especially Ziggy, still were poisonously hung over the next night during their concert at the Blaisdell Center.

Which muted their performance to a degree, a huge disappointment to Daniels who had arranged for surviving original Doors members, guitarist Robby Krieger and drummer

John Densmore, to attend and join them for a rousing version of *Light My Fire* to close the show.

The appearance of Densmore with Krieger was notable because Densmore had a long history of legal disputes with the now-deceased keyboardist Ray Manzarek and Krieger for continuing to use The Doors' name, which Densmore claimed was a violation of a 1971 agreement made after the death of Morrison that called for unanimity on partnership decisions and did not allow individual band members to use the group name.

The attorney who negotiated the ceasefire?

The only and only John Daniels.

"Daniels here is the reason why we are all here tonight in this historic reunion of the original Doors, plus us playing with the ultimate Doors cover band that has not only become a reincarnation but an evolution of The Doors," Densmore, his arm around Krieger, said into a mic on stage. "Daniels is a helluva singer and attorney. A cruel twist of irony that Jim would come back to life disguised as a lawyer."

Densmore then announced that "The Doors will be performing with the two remaining original band members for the first time in decades, and Coffeemate will join us on some tour dates. And don't be surprised to hear Jack Daniels fronting both groups as the lead singer."

"I'm just surprised that Densmore didn't sue Daniels and Coffeemate's ass for ripping off our legacy," laughed Krieger into a mic.

"Nah, these guys brought all of us, including Jim, back to life!" said a suddenly solemn Densmore.

In one bold twin-fold stroke, Daniels further punctuated his reputation as a brilliant attorney and elevated Coffeemate's stature as contemporary quasi equals of The Doors.

"Pinch me folks," screamed Toad, tears of joy streaming down his face, the astonishment and wonder of it all settling over him like a shroud.

That signature moment was a memorable moment indelibly etched into the memory banks of every Coffeemate band member.

But for one band member by the name of Daniels, it would rank below his postcard wedding to Ashley.

Daniels and Ashley were married at the Lanikuhonu resort on the west wide of Oahu, the ideal destination for an outdoor wedding ceremony where heaven meets the earth.

Surrounded by palm trees, blue ocean and green grass, the couple exchanged vows barefoot in the sand on an intimate ocean cove with a stunning sunset in the background.

Just as they proclaimed their "I do's" the flaming sun kissed the Pacific as their lips kissed for the first time as husband and wife.

It was a setting so exquisite that not even the inappropriate Mother Wanda and Brother Charlie could fuck it up, let alone the ultra chic and sophisticated quartet of Ziggy, Toad, Bones and Pudge.

Ashley and Daniels made a gorgeous wedding couple in traditional Hawaiian wedding garb. She was incandescently beautiful in a loose, flowing white gown and a wearing a crown of flowers instead of a veil. The groom wore all white -- a linen shirt and pants with a red sash around his waist.

After the ceremony, which had a cosmic elegance, they entertained their small group of guests on a tropical landscape where Hawaiian royalty used to frolic.

"So this is what happiness feels like, huh?" Ashley whispered to Daniels during their bridal dance. "We are surrounded by paradise but more importantly, we both have found paradise in each other."

Her words flowed softly, cradled in deep love and sublime contentment.

His eyes moist with joy and his heart churning with devotion, Daniels shot her a glistening gaze of adoration and said, "Who knew that I would find the perfect lady for me at the intersection where John Daniels and Jack Daniels finally became one and the same. And as remarkable as that union is, it hardly compares to the union of you and me."

They then kissed so sweetly that it lit tapers in the sacred tabernacles of their souls. They obviously were not twin cells, but they were destined to be lifetime cellmates. This was one love affair that would not disappear like morning dew.

Somehow Daniels knew that his first wife Kate, now harping with the angels, would have approved of the John-Jack and the Daniels-Ashley mergers. But he knew that Kate would never understand how he could have forsaken his beloved Scotch and made Jack Daniels his drink of choice.

CPSIA information can be obtained at www.ICGtesting.com
Printed in the USA
BVOW08s0003140516

447801BV00001B/1/P